Alexander Agassiz, Walter Faxon

Bibliography to Accompany

Alexander Agassiz, Walter Faxon

Bibliography to Accompany

ISBN/EAN: 9783337389765

Printed in Europe, USA, Canada, Australia, Japan

Cover: Foto ©Andreas Hilbeck / pixelio.de

More available books at **www.hansebooks.com**

No. 6. — *Bibliography to accompany " Selections from Embryological Monographs" compiled by* Alexander Agassiz, Walter Faxon, *and* E. L. Mark.

I.

CRUSTACEA.

By Walter Faxon.

[It is proposed to issue in the Memoirs of the Museum a "Selection from Embryological Monographs," which will give to the student, in an easily accessible form, a more or less complete iconography of the embryology of each important group of the animal kingdom. This selection is not intended to be a handbook, but rather an atlas to accompany any general work on the subject.

The plates will be issued in parts, as fast as practicable, each part covering a somewhat limited field. The parts devoted to Echinoderms, Acalephs, and Polyps are well advanced, and a beginning has been made for the Crustacea. Occasional appendices may be published, to prevent the plates from becoming antiquated.

The quarto illustrations will be accompanied by a carefully prepared explanation, and by a bibliography, in octavo, to be made as complete as possible. Although a large part of this bibliographical literature may be found in the general works of Kölliker, Balbiani, and Balfour, and in some of the more recent special monographs, a fuller list on special subjects, comprising the scattered references now accessible only with much cost of time and labor, will be convenient for students.

The present Bulletin contains the first instalment of this bibliography. It will be followed at an early date by similar lists for the Echinoderms, the Acalephs, the Polyps, and the Fishes.   ALEXANDER AGASSIZ.

The embryological literature of the Arthropod groups *incertæ sedis*, viz. *Xiphosura, Trilobita*, and *Pycnogonida*, will be found at the end of this list. An asterisk (*) before a title denotes that the work cited has not been seen by me.

December 3, 1881.   W. F.]

Agassiz, Alexander.
 [On the Development of the *Porcellanidæ*.]   *Proc. Boston Soc. Nat. Hist.*, X. p. 222.   Oct. 18, *1865*.
 (Zoëa of *Porcellana (Polyonyx) macrocheles* recorded from Newport, R. I.)

 Instinct ? in Hermit Crabs.   *Amer. Journ. Sci. & Arts* [3], X. pp. 290, 291. Oct. *1875*.
                         (Habits of young.)

Agassiz, Louis.
 Twelve Lectures on Comparative Embryology, delivered before the Lowell Institute, in Boston, December and January, 1848–49.   Boston, *1849*. 104 pp.

   (Eggs of *Pinnotheres*, p. 67, Pl. XXII.   Development of *Palæmon*, pp. 67, 68, Pl. III.   *Cumæ* the young of *Palæmon, Hippolyte*, and *Mysis*, p. 68.)

Zoölogical Notes from the Correspondence of Prof. Agassiz. *Amer. Journ. Sci. & Arts* [2], XIII. pp. 425, 426, *1852;* XXII. pp. 285, 286, *1856.*

(*Cumæ* the young of *Crangon, Palæmon,* and *Hippolyte.*)

Allman [George James].

On the Development of *Notodelphys,* Allm., a new Genus of *Entomostraca. Rep. Brit. Assoc. Adv. Sci. for* 1847, p. 74. *1848.*

Anderson, John.

On the Anatomy of *Sacculina,* with a Description of the Species. *Ann. Mag. Nat. Hist.* [3], IX. pp. 12–19, Pl. I. *1862.*

(Larva, pp. 13, 14, fig. 1.)

Aurivillius, P. O. Christopher.

On a new Genus and Species of *Harpacticida. Bihang till K. Svenska Vetensk.- Akad. Handl.,* V. No. 18. *1879.* 14 pp., 4 pl.

(*Balænophilus unisetus.* Development, pp. 10–15, Pl. III., IV.)

*Balaenophilus unisetus nov. Gen. et Sp. Ett Bidrag till Kännedomen om Harpacticidernas Utvecklingshistoria och Systematik. Stockholm, *1879.* 26 pp., 4 pl. (Akadem. Afhandl.)

Baird, W.

The Natural History of the British *Entomostraca.* London, *1850.* 364 pp., 36 pl.

Previously in *Mag. Zoöl. Bot.,* I. pp. 35–41, 309–333, 514–526, Pl. VIII.–X., XVI., *1837;* II. pp. 132–144, 400–412, Pl. V., *1838. Ann. Nat. Hist.,* I. pp. 245–256, Pl. IX., *1838. Ann. Mag. Nat. Hist.,* XI. pp. 81–95, Pl. II., III., *1843.*

(Young stages, *passim.*)

Balbiani [G.].

Observations relatives à une Note récente de M. Gerbe, sur la Constitution et le Développement de l'Œuf ovarien des Sacculines. *Comptes Rendus de l'Acad. des Sci., Paris,* LXVIII. pp. 615–618. *1869.*

Sur la Constitution et le Mode de Formation de l'Œuf des Sacculines. *Comptes Rendus de l'Acad. des Sci., Paris,* LXIX. pp. 1320–1324. *1869. Ann. Mag. Nat. Hist.* [4], V. pp. 303–306. *1870.*

Sur la Constitution et le Mode de Formation de l'Œuf des Sacculines. Remarques concernant une Note récente de M. Ed. Van Beneden. *Comptes Rendus de l'Acad. des Sci., Paris,* LXIX. pp. 1376–1379. *1869.*

Balfour, Francis M.

A Treatise on Comparative Embryology. Vol. I. Chapter XVIII. Crustacea. Pp. 380–443. London, *1880.*

(General work.)

Bate, C. Spence.

Notes on Crustacea. *Ann. Mag. Nat. Hist.* [2], VI. pp. 109–111, Pl. VII. *1850.*

> (On the mode of escape of *Pagurus* larva from the egg, p. 111.)

On the Development of the *Cirripedia*. *Ann. Mag. Nat. Hist.* [2], VIII. pp. 324–332, Pl. VI.–VIII. *1851.*

On the British *Edriophthalmia*. Part I. The *Amphipoda*. *Rep. Brit. Assoc. Adv. Sci. for* 1855. *1856.*

> (On the development of the young, pp. 55, 56.)

On the British *Diastylidæ*. *Ann. Mag. Nat. Hist.* [2], XVII. pp. 449–465, Pl. XIII.–XV. *1856.*

> (On the development, p. 463. Zoëa of *Hippolyte varians*, pp. 461, 462, Pl. XV. fig. 8.)

On the Development of *Carcinus Mænas*. *Proc. Roy. Soc. London*, VIII. pp. 544–546. *1857.*

> (Abstract of paper given in full in *Phil. Trans. Roy. Soc. London*. CXLVIII.)

On the Genus *Cuma*. *Ann. Mag. Nat. Hist.* [2], XIX. pp. 106, 107. *1857.*

> (On the affinity of *Cumæ* with young *Macroura*.)

On *Praniza* and *Anceus*, and their Affinity to each other. *Ann. Mag. Nat. Hist.* [3], II. pp. 165–172, Pl. VI., VII. *1858.*

On the Development of Decapod Crustacea. *Phil. Trans. Roy. Soc. London*, CXLVIII. pp. 589–605, Pl. XL.–XLVI. *1859.* (Received May 1, read June 18, 1857.)

> (Development of *Carcinus Mænas*.)

On the Morphology of some *Amphipoda* of the Division *Hyperina*. *Ann. Mag. Nat. Hist.* [3], VIII. pp. 1–16, Pl. I., II. *1861.*

> (Young described.)

[Review of Fritz Müller's *Für Darwin*.] *Rec. Zoölog. Lit.* (1864), I. pp. 261–270. *1865.*

[Review of Z. Gerbe's *Métamorphoses des Crustacés marins*.] *Rec. Zoölog. Lit.* (1865), II. pp. 321, 322. *1866.*

Report of the Committee appointed to explore the Marine Fauna and Flora of the South Coast of Devon and Cornwall. No. 1. *Rep. Brit. Assoc. Adv. Sci. for* 1865. *1866.*

> (*Glaucothoë* the young of *Pagurus*, p. 53.)

Also published with title, Carcinological Gleanings, No. II., in *Ann. Mag. Nat. Hist.* [3], XVII. p. 26. *1866.*

Carcinological Gleanings. No. III. *Ann. Mag. Nat. Hist.* [4], I. pp. 442–448, Pl. XXI. *1868.*

> (Believes *Alima* to be the second stage of *Squilla*. Young of *Uca*, see CUNNINGHAM, ROBERT O.)

Report of the Committee appointed to explore the Marine Fauna and Flora of the South Coast of Devon and Cornwall. No. 2. *Rep. Brit. Assoc. Adv. Sci. for* 1867. *1868.*

> (Larvæ of *Porcellana, Pagurus, Palinurus*, pp. 279-282, Pl. I., II.)

Also published with title, Carcinological Gleanings, No. IV., in *Ann. Mag. Nat. Hist.* [4], II. pp. 113-117, Pl. IX., X. *1868.*

Fourth Report on the Fauna of South Devon. *Rep. Brit. Assoc. Adv. Sci. for* 1872. *1873.*

> (Observation on the development of *Homarus*, &c., p. 52.)

Report on the Present State of our Knowledge of the Crustacea.   Parts I. and II. On the Homologies of the Dermal Skeleton. *Rep. Brit. Assoc. Adv. Sci. for* 1875, pp. 41-53, Pl. I., II. *1876. Do. for* 1876, pp. 75-94, Pl. II., III. *1877.*

> (Remarks on development, *passim.*)

On the Nauplius Stage of Prawns. *Ann. Mag. Nat. Hist.* [5], II. pp. 79-85. *1878.*

> *   (Thinks Fritz Müller's "*Peneus*-nauplius" may be a larval Schizopod or parasitic Suctorian. Larva of *Galatea* noticed, p. 82.)

Report on the Present State of our Knowledge of the Crustacea.   Part IV. On Development. *Rep. Brit. Assoc. Adv. Sci. for* 1878, pp. 193-209, Pl. V.-VII. *1879.*

> (*Gelasimus, Trapezia, Dromia, Porcellana, Galatea, Astacus, Crangon, Palæmon*, &c.)

Report on the Present State of our Knowledge of the Crustacea.   Part V. On Fecundation, Respiration, and the Green Gland. *Rep. Brit. Assoc. Adv. Sci. for* 1880, pp. 230-241. *1880.*

> (Account of recent observations of CHANTRAN, GERBE, WILLEMOES-SUHM, &c.)

On the *Penæidea*. *Ann. Mag. Nat. Hist.* [5], VIII. pp. 169-196, Pl. XI., XII. *1881.*

> (Genus *Euphema* M. Edw. a young form of *Peneus?* p. 192.)

Bate (C. Spence) and Müller (Fritz).
The Nauplius Stage of Prawns. *Ann. Mag. Nat. Hist.* [5], II. pp. 426, 427. *1878.*

Bate, C. Spence [and Power, Wilmot Henry].
On the Development of the Crustacean Embryo, and the Variations of Form exhibited in the Larvæ of thirty-eight Genera of Podophthalmia. *Proc. Roy. Soc. London,* XXIV. pp. 375-379. *1876. Ann. Mag. Nat. Hist.* [4], XVIII. pp. 174-177. *1876.*

Bate (C. Spence) and Westwood (J. O.).
A History of the British Sessile-eyed Crustacea. 2 vols. London, *1861-1868.* lvi. + 507 + 536 pp.

> (Observations on development, pp. xliii.-xlvi., *1868* (C. S. Bate), *et passim.*)

Bell, Thomas.

A History of the British Stalk-eyed Crustacea. London, *1853.* lxv. + 386 pp.

(Metamorphosis, pp. xxxviii.-lxi., *et passim.*)

Beneden. *See* **Van Beneden.**

Bessels, Emil.

Einige Worte über die Entwickelungsgeschichte und den morphologischen Werth des kugelförmigen Organes der Amphipoden. *Jenaische Zeitschr.,* V. pp. 91–101. *1870.*

See also **Van Beneden, Édouard.**

Birge, Edward A.

Notes on *Cladocera. Trans. Wisconsin Acad. Sci., Arts, & Letters,* IV. pp. 77–112, Pl. I., II. *1878.*

(Some notes on young, *passim.*)

Boas, J. E. V.

Amphion und *Polycheles* (*Willemoesia*). *Zoolog. Anzeig.,* II. pp. 256–259. May, *1879.*

(*Amphion* the larva of *Polycheles?*)

Studier over Decapodernes Slægtskabsforhold. Avec un Résumé en français. *K. Danske Vidensk. Selsk. Skr.* [6], *naturvidensk. og mathemat. Afd.* I. pp. 25–210, 7 pl. *1880.*

Abstr. in *Journ. Roy. Microscop. Soc.* [2], I. pp. 450–452. *1881.*

(Development, *passim.*)

Bobretzky, N.

K Embriologii Tshlenistonogikh [On the Embryology of Arthropods]. *Zapiski Kiefskavo Obshtchestva Yestestvoispitatalyei,* III., *1873.* [*Mem. Kieff Naturalists' Soc.,* III. pp. 129–263, Pl. I.-VI. *1873.*]

Abstr. in German by HOYER in *Hofmann u. Schwalbe's Jahresberichte,* II. pp. 31–2318. *1875.*

(*Astacus* and *Palæmon.*)

Zur Embryologie des *Oniscus murarius. Zeitschr. f. wissensch. Zool.,* XXIV. pp. 179–203, Taf. XXI., XXII. *1874.*

Boeck, Axel.

Om det norske Hummerfiski og dets Historie. Tidsskrift for Fiskeri, Kjobenhavn, 3^{die} Aargangs, pp. 28–43, *1868 ;* pp. 145–189, *1869.*

Translated in *United States Commission of Fish and Fisheries,* Part III. *Report of the Commissioner for* 1873–74 *and* 1874–75, pp. 223–258. *1876.*

(Observations on development of *Homarus,* pp. 226, 227.)

Bosc, L. A. G.

Histoire Naturelle des Crustacés. Paris, *1802.*

(Genus *Zoëa* founded for reception of the Brachyuran larva described by SLABBER under the name of *Monoculus taurus.*)

Bovallius, Carl.

Embryologiska Studier. I. Om Balanidernas Utveckling. Stockholm, *1875.* 44 pp., 5 pl.

Brandt, Eduard.

Ueber die Jungen der gemeinen Klappenassel (*Idothea entomon*). *Bull. Acad. Impér. des Sci. de St.-Pétersbourg*, XV. pp. 403–409 (*Mélanges Biologiques*, VII. pp. 649–657), 1 pl. *1870.*

Brauer, Friedrich.

Beiträge zur Kenntniss der Phyllopoden. *Sitzungsber. d. kais. Akad. d. Wissensch. Wien. Math.-naturw. Cl.*, LXV. pp. 279–291. *1872.*

Abstr. *Anzeiger d. Akad. d. Wissensch. Wien*, May 31, 1872, p. 100. *Ann. Mag. Nat. Hist.* [4] X. p. 152, *1872.* **Zeitschr. gesammt. Naturwissen.* [2], VI. pp. 314, 315, *1872.*

(Parthenogenesis of *Apus*, &c.)

Vorläufige Mittheilungen über die Entwicklung und Lebensweise des *Lepidurus productus* Bosc. *Sitzungsber. d. kais. Akad. d. Wissensch. Wien. Math.-naturw. Cl.*, LXIX., I. Abt. pp. 130–140, Taf. I., II. *1874.*

Bree, W. T.

Ecdysis, or the Casting of the Skin or Shell, in Crustaceous Animals. *Mag. Nat. Hist. (Loudon's)*, VIII. pp. 468, 469. August, *1835.*

(*Astacus* hatched in the adult form.)

Brightwell, T.

Description of the Young of the Common Lobster, with Observations relative to the Questions of the Occurrence and Non-occurrence of Transformations in Crustaceous Animals. *Mag. Nat. Hist. (Loudon's)*, VIII. pp. 482–486. September, *1835*

(*Homarus, Astacus.*)

Brooks, W. K.

The Larval Stages of *Squilla Empusa* Say. *Chesapeake Zoölogical Laboratory. Scientific Results of the Session of* 1878, pp. 143–170, Pl. IX.–XIII. February, *1879.*

Also published as *Studies from the Biological Laboratory of Johns Hopkins University*, I. Part 3.

The Rhythmical Character of the Process of Segmentation. *Amer. Journ. Sci. & Arts* [3], XX. p. 293. October, *1880.*

(Observed in eggs of *Lucifer*.)

The Young of the Crustacean *Lucifer*, a Nauplius. *Amer. Naturalist*, XIV. pp. 806–808. November, *1880.*

(Also records obs. of E. B. WILSON that zoëa of *Libinia* has full number of thoracic appendages when it leaves egg. WILSON has also raised zoëa from eggs of *Porcellana, Pinnixa, Sesarma, Pinnotheres*, and *Callinectes*.)

The Embryology and Metamorphosis of the *Sergestidæ*. *Zoolog. Anzeig.*, III. pp. 563–567, 15 Nov., *1880.*

Also brief notice in *Fifth Annual Report of the Johns Hopkins University*. *Baltimore, Maryland*, 1880, Appendix F, " Report of Chesapeake Zoölogical Laboratory for the Third Year, Summer of 1880, Beaufort, N. C.," p. 57. *1880*.

(*Lucifer, Acetes?*)

Lucifer : a Study in Morphology. (Abstract.) *Proc. Roy. Soc. London*, No. 212, *1881*. 3 pp.

(Development of *Lucifer, Acetes ?*)

Brooks (W. K.) and Wilson (E. B.).

The First Zoëa of Porcellana. *Studies from the Biological Laboratory of Johns Hopkins University*, II. No. 1, pp. 58–64, Pl. VI., VII. *1881*.

Buchholz, Reinhold.

Ueber *Hemioniscus*, eine neue Gattung parasitischer Isopoden. *Zeitschr. f. wissensch. Zool.*, XVI. pp. 303–327, Taf. XVI., XVII. *1866*.

Beiträge zur Kenntniss der innerhalb der Ascidien lebenden parasitischen Crustaceen des Mittelmeeres. *Zeitschr. f. wissensch. Zool.*, XIX. pp. 99–155, Taf. V.–XI. *1869*.

(Figures nauplii of several *Notodelphyidæ*.)

See also **Münter, Jul.**

Bullar, J. F.

On the Development of the Parasitic *Isopoda*. *Phil. Trans. Roy. Soc. London*, CLXIX. pp. 505–521, Pl. XLV.–XLVII. *1878*. Abstr. in *Proc. Roy. Soc. London*, XXVII. pp. 284–286. April 4, *1878*.

(*Cymothoë*.)

Burmeister, Hermann.

Beiträge zur Naturgeschichte der Rankenfüsser (*Cirripedia*). Berlin, *1834*. viii. + 60 pp., 2 pl.

(Development, pp. 12-27, Pl. I.)

Cane. *See* **DuCane.**

Carbonnier, Pierre.

L'Écrevisse. Mœurs — Reproduction — Education. Paris, *1869*. 197 pp.

(Notes on hatching and young. Ch. VI. pp. 49-56.)

Cavolini, Filippo.

*Memoria sulla Generazione dei Pesci e dei Granchi. Napoli. *1787*.

Germ. transl. by E. A. W. ZIMMERMANN. Abhandlung über die Erzeugung der Fische und der Krebse. Berlin, *1792*. 192 pp., 3 pl.

(Zoëa of *Brachyura* [*Grapsus varius ?*], young of *Entoniscus, Rhizocephala*, &c.)

Chantran, Samuel.

Observations sur l'Histoire Naturelle des Écrevisses. *Comptes Rendus de l'Acad. des Sci., Paris*, LXXI. pp. 43–45. *1870*

Trans. in *Ann. Mag. Nat. Hist.* [4]. VI. pp. 265–267. *1870*. *Journ. de l'Anat. et de la Physiol.* (*Robin's*), VIII. pp. 236–238. *1872*. *Rev. Mag. Zool.* [2], XXIII. pp. 75-78. *1871-72*.

Nouvelles Observations sur le Développement des Écrevisses. *Comptes Rendus de l'Acad. des Sci., Paris,* LXXIII. pp. 220, 221. *1871.*

Trans. in *Ann. Mag. Nat. Hist.* [4], VIII. pp. 219, 220. *1871. Journ. de l'Anat. et de la Physiol.* (*Robin's*), VIII. p. 238. *1872. Rev. Mag. Zool.* [2], XXIII. pp. 78, 79. *1871-72.*

Claparède, A. René Edouard.

Beobachtungen über Anatomie und Entwicklungsgeschichte wirbelloser Thiere an der Küste von Normandie angestellt. Leipzig, *1863.* viii. + 120 pp., 18 pl.

(Development of *Mysis,* pp. 92-94, Pl. XVII. figs. 1-6; *Lepas anatifera,* pp. 98-101, Pl. XVII. figs. 15-26; *Phoxichilidium,* pp. 104, 105, Pl. XVIII. figs. 13, 14.)

Claus, Carl.

Ueber den Bau und die Entwickelung parasitischer Crustaceen. Cassel, *1858.* 34 pp., 2 pl.

(*Chondracanthus, Lernanthropus, Kroyeria.*)

Zur Anatomie und Entwickelungsgeschichte der Copepoden. *Arch. f. Naturgesch.,* XXIV. 1, pp. 1-76, Taf. I.-III. *1858.*

*Zur Kenntniss der Malacostracenlarven. *Würzburg. naturwiss. Zeitschr.,* II. pp. 23-46. *1861.*

Ueber die morphologischen Beziehungen der Copepoden zu den verwandten Crustaceengruppen der Malacostraken, Phyllopoden, Cirripedien und Ostracoden. *Würzburg. naturwiss. Zeitschr.,* III. pp. 159-167. *1862.*

Ueber den Bau und die Entwicklung von *Achtheres percarum. Zeitschr. f. wissensch. Zool.,* XI. pp. 287-308, Taf. XXIII., XXIV. *1862.*

Die frei lebenden Copepoden mit besonderer Berücksichtigung der Fauna Deutschlands, der Nordsee und des Mittelmeeres. Leipzig, *1863.* x. + 230 pp., 37 pl.

(Development, pp. 72-83. Figures several nauplii.)

Ueber einige Schizopoden und niedere Malacostraken Messina's. *Zeitschr. f. wissensch. Zool.,* XIII. pp. 422-454, Taf. XXV.-XXIX. *1863.*

(Development of *Palinurus, Sergestes, Euphausia.*)

Zur näheren Kenntniss der Jugendformen von *Cypris ovum. Zeitschr. f. wissensch. Zool.,* XV. pp. 391-398, Taf. XXVIII., XXIX. *1865.*

Abstr. by C. Spence Bate in *Rec. Zoöl. Lit.* (1865), II. pp. 344, 345. *1866.*

Die Copepoden-Fauna von Nizza. Ein Beitrag zur Charakteristik der Formen und deren Abänderungen "im Sinne Darwin's." *Schriften d. Gesell. zur Beförderung d. gesammt. Naturwissen. zu Marburg,* IX. Suppl. 1. 34 pp., 5 pl. *1866.*

(Young *Calanella,* p. 9, Taf. V. fig. 22. *Calanus mastigophorus?* pp. 10, 11, Taf. V. figs. 20, 21.)

Ueber *Lernaeocera esocina* v. Nordm. (Vorläufige Mittheilung.) *Sitzungsber. d. Gesell. zur Beförderung d. gesammt. Naturwissen. zu Marburg, 1867,* pp. 5–12.

(Development, pp. 11, 12.)

Ueber den Entwicklungsmodus der *Porcellana*-Larven im Vergleiche zu den Larven von *Pagurus. Sitzungsber. der Gesell. zur Beförderung d. gesammt. Naturwissen. zu Marburg, 1867,* pp. 12–16.

Ueber die Metamorphose und systematische Stellung der Lernaeen. *Sitzungsber. d. Gesell. zur Beförderung d. gesammt. Naturwissen. zu Marburg, 1868,* pp. 5–13.

Beiträge zur Kenntniss der Ostracoden. I. Entwicklungsgeschichte von *Cypris. Schriften d. Gesell. zur Beförderung d. gesammt. Naturwissen. zu Marburg,* IX. pp. 151–166, 2 pl. *1868.*

> Abstr. in *Ann. Mag. Nat. Hist.* [4], IV. pp. 291, 292. *1869.* *Arch. *Sci. Phys.,* XXXV. pp. 312–314. *1869.*

Beobachtungen über *Lernaeocera, Peniculus* und *Lernaea.* Ein Beitrag zur Naturgeschichte der Lernaeen. *Schriften d. Gesell. zur Beförderung d. gesammt. Naturwissen. zu Marburg,* IX. Suppl. 2. 32 pp., 4 pl. *1868.*

> (Young of *Lernaeocera esocina.* Metamorphosis of *Lernaea branchialis,* pp. 16–27, Taf. IV.)

Die *Cypris*-ähnliche Larve (Puppe) der Cirripedien und ihre Verwandlung in das festsitzende Thier. Ein Beitrag zur Morphologie der Rankenfüssler. *Schriften d. Gesell. zur Beförderung d. gesammt. Naturwissen. zu Marburg,* IX. Suppl. 5. 17 pp., 2 pl. *1869.*

Die Metamorphose der Squilliden. *Nachrichten Kön. Gesell. Wissensch. Göttingen, 1871,* pp. 169–180. (Abstract.) *Abh. Kön. Gesell. Wissensch. Göttingen,* XVI. pp. 111–163, Taf. I.–VIII. *1871.* (Full memoir.)

Zur Kenntniss des Bau's und der Entwicklung von *Apus* und *Branchipus. Nachrichten Kön. Gesell. Wissensch. Göttingen, 1872,* pp. 209–225. *Zeitschr. gesammt. Naturwissen.,* VI. pp. 200, 201. *1872.*

Zur Kenntniss des Baues und der Entwicklung von *Branchipus stagnalis* und *Apus cancriformis. Abh. Kön. Gesell. Wissensch. Göttingen,* XVIII. pp. 93–140, Taf. I.–VIII. *1873.*

Ueber die Entwickelung, Organisation und systematische Stellung der Arguliden. *Zeitschr. f. wissensch. Zool.,* XXV., pp. 217–284, Taf. XIV.–XVIII. *1875.*

*Das System der Crustaceen im Lichte der Descendenzlehre. I. Die Metamorphose der Malakostraken. Wien, *1875.*

Zur Kenntniss der Organisation und des feinern Baues der Daphniden und verwandter Cladoceren. *Zeitschr. f. wissensch. Zool.,* XXVII. pp. 362–402, Taf. XXV.–XXVIII. Aug., *1876.*

> (Structure of ovary, eggs, &c., pp. 389–399, Taf. XXVII. figs. 15–20.)

Grundzüge der Zoologie. Zum Gebrauche an Universitäten und höheren Lehranstalten sowie zum Selbststudium. 3te Aufl. Marburg und Leipzig, *1874, 1876.* xii. + 1254 pp.

(Development of Crustacea, pp. 450-562, *passim. 1876.*)

Untersuchungen zur Erforschung der Genealogischen Grundlage des Crustaceen-Systems. Ein Beitrag zur Descendenzlehre. Wien, *1876.* viii. + 114 pp., 19 pl.

Noticed by EDUARD VON MARTENS in *Zoolog. Rec.* (1876), XIII. *Crust.*, pp. 2, 3. *1878.*

(General work on development of Crustacea.)

Neue Beiträge zur Kenntniss der Copepoden unter besonderer Berücksichtigung der Triester Fauna. *Arbeiten aus d. zoolog. Inst. d. Universität Wien u. d. zoolog. Station in Triest,* III. pp. 313-332, Taf. XXIII.-XXV. *1881.*

(Young males of certain species resemble the female in the segmentation of the antennæ, &c.)

Coldstream, John.

On the Structure and Habits of the *Limnoria terebrans,* a minute Crustaceous Animal, destructive to marine wooden Erections, as Piers, &c. *Edinburgh New Philosoph. Journ.,* XVI. pp. 316-334, Pl. VI. *1834.*

(Young, p. 325, Pl. VI. figs. 17, 18.)

Cornalia (Emilio) and Panceri (Paolo).

Osservazioni zoologico-anatomiche sopra un nuovo Genere di Crostacei Isopodi sedentarii (*Gyge branchialis*). *Memorie della Reale Accad. d. Scienze di Torino,* [2], XIX. *1858.* 36 pp., 2 pl.

(Development, pp. 21-27, Pl. I. figs. 6-25.)

Costa, Oronzio-Gabriele.

Fauna del Regno di Napoli, &c. Napoli, *1829, et seqq.*

(Embryo of *Callianassa subterranea,* Decapodi Macrouri, Tav. I^bis, fig. 2, pp. 9, 10. Feb. *1847.*)

A few plates are missing from the copy of this work in the library of the Museum of Comparative Zoölogy. According to Leuckart, *Arch. f. Naturgesch.,* 1859, 1, p. 246, the embryo of *Notopterophorus* is figured.

Coste [P.].

Note sur la Larve des Langoustes. *Comptes Rendus de l'Acad. des Sci., Paris,* XLVI. pp. 547, 548. *1858. Ann. Mag. Nat. Hist.* [3], 1. p. 466. *1858.*

(*Phyllosoma* the larva of *Palinurus.*)

Études sur les Mœurs et sur la Génération d'un certain Nombre d'Animaux marins. *Comptes Rendus de l'Acad. des Sci., Paris,* XLVII. pp. 45-50. *1858.*

Trans. in *Ann. Mag. Nat. Hist.* [3], II. pp. 197-202. *1858.*

Couch, R. Q.

On the Metamorphoses of the Decapod Crustaceans. *The Eleventh Annual Report of the Royal Cornwall Polytechnic Society, 1843,* pp. 28–43, Pl. I. Falmouth.

(*Carcinus Mænas, Portunus plicatus, Cancer pagurus, Maia verrucosa, Inachus dorynchus, Pisa Gibbsii, Homarus vulgaris, Palinurus vulgaris, Galatea squamifera. Xantho floridus, X. rivulosus, Pilumnus hirtellus, Polybius Henslowii, Portunus puber,* and several others hatched as zoëæ.)

See BELL's *Hist. Brit. Stalk-eyed Crustacea.* London, *1853.*

On the Metamorphosis of the Crustaceans, including the *Decapoda, Entomostraca,* and *Pycnogonidæ. The Twelfth Annual Report of the Royal Cornwall Polytechnic Society, 1844,* pp. 17–46, Pl. I. Falmouth.

(*Carcinus Mænas, Palinurus vulgaris, Homarus vulgaris, Crangon vulgaris, Palæmon serratus, Porcellana platycheles, Cyclops quadricornis, Orithyia coccinea, Nymphon gracile.*)

See BELL's *Hist. Brit. Stalk-eyed Crustacea.* London, *1853.*

[Letter to C. Spence Bate on the Larvæ of *Cuma.*] *Ann. Mag. Nat. Hist.* [2], XIX. pp. 106, 107. *1857.*

On the Embryo State of *Palinurus vulgaris. Nat. Hist. Rev.,* IV., Proc. Soc., pp. 250–257, Pl. XVII. *1857. Rep. Brit. Assoc. Adv. Sci. for* 1857, Trans. of Sect., pp. 102, 103. *1858.*

(Larva referred to *Phyllosoma* by GERSTAECKER, *Arch. f. Naturgesch. 1858,* 2, p. 455.)

Cunningham, Robert O.

[Letter to C. Spence Bate,] Carcinological Gleanings, No. III., *Ann. Mag. Nat. Hist.* [4], I. pp. 442–446. *1868.*

(*Uca Cunninghami* Bate with live, fully developed young ones under the pleon.)

Czerniavsky. *See* **Tscherniawsky.**

Dana, James D.

United States Exploring Expedition, during the Years 1838, 1839, 1840, 1841, 1842, under the Command of Charles Wilkes, U. S. N. Vol. XIII. Crustacea. Philadelphia, *1852.* xii. + 1618 pp., 96 pl.

(*Passim.*)

Danielssen [D. C.]. *See* **Koren, J.**

Darwin, Charles.

A Monograph on the Sub-Class *Cirripedia,* with Figures of all the Species. The *Lepadidæ,* or Pedunculated Cirripedes. London, *1851.* xii. + 400 pp., 10 pl.

(Metamorphoses, pp. 8–23.)

The *Balanidæ,* or Sessile Cirripedes, the *Verrucidæ,* &c., &c. London, *1854.* viii. + 684 pp., 30 pl.

(Metamorphoses, pp. 102–133.)

De Filippi. *See* Filippi.

De Geer. *See* Geer.

De La Valette St. George. *See* La Valette St. George.

Dohrn, Anton.

Die embryonale Entwicklung des *Asellus aquaticus.* *Zeitschr. f. wissensch. Zool.,* XVII. pp. 221–278, Pl. XIV., XV. *1867.*

On the Morphology of the Arthropoda. *Journ. of Anat. and Physiol.,* II. ([2], I.) pp. 80–86. *1868.*

> Abstr. in *Rep. Brit. Assoc. Adv. Sci. for* 1867, Trans. of Sect., p. 82. *1868.*

Untersuchungen über Bau und Entwickelung der Arthropoden. 1. Ueber den Bau und die Entwickelung der Cumaceen. *Jenaische Zeitschr.,* V. pp. 54–81, Taf. II., III. *1870.*

Untersuchungen über Bau und Entwicklung der Arthropoden. 3. Die Schalendrüse und die embryonale Entwicklung der Daphnien. *Jenaische Zeitschr.,* V. pp. 277–306, Taf. X. *1870.*

Untersuchungen über Bau und Entwicklung der Arthropoden. 4. Entwicklung und Organisation von *Praniza (Anceus) maxillaris.* *Zeitschr. f. wissensch. Zool.,* XX. pp. 55–80, Taf. VI.–VIII. *1869.*

Untersuchungen über Bau und Entwicklung der Arthropoden. 5. Zur Kentniss des Baues von *Paranthura Costana.* *Zeitschr. f. wissensch. Zool.,* XX. pp. 81–93, Taf. IX. *1869.*

> (Observations on development in *Nachtrag.*)

Untersuchungen über Bau und Entwicklung der Arthropoden. 6. Zur Entwicklungsgeschichte der Panzerkrebse (*Decapoda Loricata*). *Zeitschr. f. wissensch. Zool.,* XX. pp. 249–271, Taf. XVI. *1870.*

> (*Scyllarus arctus, Palinurus vulgaris.*)

Untersuchungen über Bau und Entwicklung der Arthropoden. 7. Zur Kenntniss vom Bau und der Entwicklung von *Tanais.* *Jenaische Zeitschr.,* V. pp. 293–306, Taf. XI., XII. *1870.*

Untersuchungen über Bau und Entwicklung der Arthropoden. 8. Die Ueberreste des Zoëa-Stadiums in der ontogenetischen Entwicklung der verschiedenen Crustaceen-Familien. *Jenaische Zeitschr.,* V. pp. 471–491. *1870.*

Untersuchungen über Bau und Entwicklung der Arthropoden. 9. Eine neue Nauplius-Form (*Archizoëa gigas*). *Zeitschr. f. wissensch. Zool.,* XX. pp. 597–606, Taf. XXVIII., XXIX. *1870.*

> (*Cirripedia.*)

Untersuchungen über Bau und Entwicklung der Arthropoden. 10. Beiträge zur Kenntniss der Malacostraken und ihrer Larven. *Zeitschr. f. wissensch. Zool.,* XX. pp. 607–626, Taf. XXX.–XXXII. *1870.*

> (*Amphion, Lophogaster, Portunus, Pandalus, Galatea, Elaphocaris.*)

Untersuchungen über Bau und Entwicklung der Arthropoden. 11. Zweiter Beitrag zur Kenntniss der Malacostraken und ihrer Larven-formen. *Zeitschr. f. wissensch. Zool.*, XXI. pp. 356–379, Taf. XXVII.–XXX. *1871.*

(Zoëæ, pp. 372–378, Taf. XXIX., XXX.)

Geschichte des Krebsstammes, nach embryologischen, anatomischen und palaeontologischen Quellen. *Jenaische Zeitschr.*, VI. pp. 96–156. *1871.*

Der Ursprung der Wirbelthiere und das Princip des Functionswechsels. Genealogische Skizzen. Leipzig, *1875.* 87 pp.

(Contains remarks on development of various Crustacea, *passim.*)

DuCane, C.

Letter from Captain DuCane, R. N., to the Rev. Leonard Jenyns, on the subject of the Metamorphosis of Crustacea. Extract from a Letter on the same subject from Captain DuCane, R. N., to W. S. MacLeay, Esq. *Ann. Nat. Hist.*, II. pp. 178–181, Pl. VI., VII. *1839.*

(*Palæmon, Crangon.*)

On the Metamorphoses of the Crustacea. *Ann. Nat. Hist.*, III. pp. 438–440, Pl. XI. *1839.*

(*Carcinus Mænas.*)

Dujardin, Félix.

Observations sur les Métamorphoses de la *Porcellana longicornis*, et Description de la Zoé, qui est la Larve de ce Crustacé. *Comptes Rendus de l'Acad. des Sci., Paris*, XVI. pp. 1204–1207. *1843.*

Duthiers. *See* **Lacaze-Duthiers.**

Edwards. *See* **Milne Edwards.**

Erdl, M. P.

Entwicklung des Hummereies von den ersten Veränderungen im Dotter an bis zur Reife des Embryo. München, *1843.* 40 pp., 4 pl.

Noticed in *Ann. Mag. Nat. Hist.*, XIII. pp. 213, 214. *1844.*

(Plate II. figs. 1–10, *Carcinus Mænas in ovo.*)

Eschscholtz, Fr.

Bericht über die zoologische Ausbeute während der Reise von Kronstadt bis St. Peter-und-Paul. *Isis, 1825*, 1, col. 733–747, Taf. V.

(*Lonchophorus anceps*, col. 734, Taf. V. fig. 1, described as a Macrouran, is a Brachyuran zoëa, described by A. Dohrn, *Zeitschr. f. wissensch. Zool.*, XXI. p. 373, Taf. XXX. fig. 52, *1871*, and by Claus, under the name of *Pluteocaris*, "Untersuchungen," &c., p. 65, Taf. XII. figs. 1–7, *1876.*)

Faxon, Walter.

On some Young Stages in the Development of *Hippa, Porcellana*, and *Pinnixa*. *Bull. Mus. Comp. Zoöl. at Harvard Coll., in Cambridge*, V. pp. 253–268, 5 pl. June 30, *1879.*

(Includes notice of unpublished observations of S. I. Smith on development of *Pinnixa*, pp. 264, 265, and *Pinnotheres*, p. 265, *foot-note.*)

On the Development of *Palæmonetes vulgaris*. *Bull. Mus. Comp. Zoöl. at Harvard Coll., in Cambridge*, V. pp. 303-330, 4 pl. Sept. *1879*.

(Includes notice of schizopod stage of *Virbius zostericola*, p. 322.)

On some Points in the Structure of the Embryonic Zoëa. *Bull. Mus. Comp. Zoöl. at Harvard Coll., in Cambridge*, VI. pp. 159-166, 2 pl. Oct. 19, *1880*.

(*Carcinus Mænas, Panopeus Sayi, Gelasimus pugnax*.)

Filippi, F. de.

Osservazioni Zoologiche. Seconda Nota sulla *Dichelaspis Darwinii*. *Archivio di Zoologia*, I. pp. 200-206, Tav. XII., XIII. *1861*.

(Development, pp. 200-203, Tav. XII., XIII. figs. 10, 11.)

*Ueber die Entwicklung von *Dichelaspis Darwinii*. *Moleschott's Untersuchungen zur Naturlehre des Menschen und der Thiere*, IX. pp. 113-120, 2 pl. *1863*.

Fischer, Sebastian.

Abhandlung über das Genus *Cypris*, und dessen in der Umgebung von St. Petersburg und von Fall bei Reval vorkommenden Arten. *Mém. des Savants étrangers prés. à l'Acad. Impér. des Sci. de St.-Pétersbourg*, VII. pp. 127-167, 11 pl. *1854*.

Also printed separately, with date *1851*.

(Young individuals of several species represented.)

Beitrag zur Kenntniss der Ostracoden. *Abhandl. d. K. bayr. Akad. d. Wissensch. München. Math. phys. Cl.*, VII. pp. 635-666, Taf. XIX., XX. *1855*.

(Young *Cypris*, pp. 643, 644, Taf. XIX. figs. 7, 8.)

Fraisse, Paul.

Die Gattung *Cryptoniscus* Fr. Müller (*Liriope* Rathke). *Arbeit. aus dem zoolog.-zootom. Inst. in Würzburg*, IV. pp. 239-296, Taf. XII.-XV. *1878*.

(Includes development. Nauplius of *Peltogaster Rodriguezii*, Taf. XV. fig. 57.)

Entoniscus Carolinii n. Sp., nebst Bemerkungen über die Umwandlung und Systematik der Bopyriden. *Arbeit. aus dem zoolog.-zootom. Inst. in Würzburg*, IV. pp. 382-440, Taf. XX., XXI. *1878*.

Frey (Heinrich) and Leuckart (Rudolph).

Beiträge zur Kenntniss wirbelloser Thiere mit besonderer Berücksichtigung der Fauna des Norddeutschen Meeres. Braunschweig, *1847*. 170 pp., 2 pl.

(Development of *Mysis*, pp. 127-130.)

Frič. *See* **Fritsch.**

Fritsch, Anton.

Ueber das Vorkommen von *Apus* und *Branchipus* in Böhmen. *Verhandl. d. Kais.-Königl. zoolog.-botan. Gesell. in Wien*, XVI. pp. 557-562. *1866*.

(On the influence of desiccation on the development of the egg, &c.)

Gamroth, Alois.

Beitrag zur Kenntniss der Naturgeschichte der Caprellen. *Zeitschr. f. wissensch. Zool.*, XXXI. 101–126, Taf. VIII.–X. *1878.*

(Development, pp. 122, 123, Taf. VIII. figs. 15–21.)

Geer, Charles De.

Mémoires pour servir à l'Histoire des Insectes. Tome VII. Stockholm, *1778.* 7e Mém. Des Monocles, pp. 443–491, Pl. XXVII.–XXX.

Germ. transl. by J. A. E. GOEZE. Abhandlungen zur Geschichte der Insekten. Bd. VII. Nürnberg, *1783.* Pp. 164–181, Pl. XXVII.–XXX.

(Larvæ of *Cladocera, Copepoda, passim.*)

Geoffroy Saint-Hilaire, Isid.

Rapport fait à l'Académie royale des Sciences, sur un Mémoire de M. Milne Edwards, intitulé : Observations sur les Changements de Forme que les Crustacés éprouvent dans le jeune Âge. *Ann. Sci. Nat.* [1], XXX. pp. 360–372. *1833.*

Gerbe, J.

Sur les *Sacculina.* Extrait d'une Lettre de M. J. Gerbe, adressée à M. Van Beneden. *Bull. Acad. Roy. Belgique*, [2], XIII. pp. 339, 340. *1862.*

(On development.)

Recherches sur la Constitution et le Développement de l'Œuf ovarien des Sacculines. *Comptes Rendus de l'Acad. des Sci., Paris*, LXVIII. pp. 460–462, 22 Feb. *1869.*

Abstr. in *Rev. Mag. Zool.* [2], XXI. pp. 79, 80. *1869.* *Ann. Mag. Nat. Hist.* [4], III. pp. 321, 322. *1869.*

Réponse aux Observations de M. Balbiani, sur le Rôle des deux Vésicules que renferme l'Œuf primitif. *Comptes Rendus de l'Acad. des Sci., Paris*, LXVIII. pp. 670, 671. Mar. 15, *1879.*

(Egg of *Sacculina.*)

Gerbe, Z.

Métamorphoses des Crustacés marins. *Comptes Rendus de l'Acad. des Sci., Paris*, LIX. pp. 1101–1103. *1864.* *Rev. Mag. Zool.* [2], XVII. pp. 79–83. *1865.* *Ann. Mag. Nat. Hist.* [3], XV. pp. 237, 238. *1865.*

Notice by C. SPENCE BATE in *Rev. Zoölog. Lit.* (1865), II. pp. 321, 322. *1866.*

(*Phyllosoma* the young of *Palinurus.* Embryonic skin with invaginated spines in numerous genera.)

Métamorphoses des Crustacés marins. Deuxième Note. *Comptes Rendus de l'Acad. des Sci., Paris*, LX. pp. 74–77. *1865.* *Rev. Mag. Zool.* [2], XVII. pp. 83–87. *1865.* *Ann. Mag. Nat. Hist.* [3], XV. pp. 356–358. *1865.*

(Internal structure of *Phyllosoma* and other larvæ.)

Appareils vasculaire et nerveux des Larves des Crustacés marins. *Comptes Rendus de l'Acad. des Sci., Paris*, LXII. pp. 932–937. Apr. 23, *1866*.
Trans. by W. S. DALLAS in *Ann. Mag. Nat. Hist.* [3], XVIII. pp. 7–12. *1866*.

(*Porcellana, Homarus, Phyllosoma, Nymphon*, &c.)

Métamorphose des Crustacés marins. Quatrième Note. *Comptes Rendus de l'Acad. des Sci., Paris*, LXII. pp. 1024–1027. May 7, *1866*. *Ann. Mag. Nat. Hist.* [3], XVIII. pp. 69–71. July, *1866*.

(Conclusions from observations recorded in three preceding notes.)

Gerstaecker, A.

Bericht über die wissenschaftlichen Leistungen im Gebiete der Entomologie während des Jahres 1857. *Arch. f. Naturgesch.* 1858, 2, p. 455.

(Larva of *Palinurus*, described by R. Q. COUCH (*Nat. Hist. Rev.* IV., *Rep. Brit. Assoc. Adv. Sci. for* 1857), referred to *Phyllosoma*.)

Vol. V. (Arthropoda) of BRONN's *Klassen und Ordnungen des Thier-Reichs*. Leipzig und Heidelberg, *1866 et seqq.*

(Development, *passim*.)

[On *Ornitholepas australis* Targ. Tozz.] *Sitz.-Ber. Gesell. naturf. Freunde zu Berlin*, *1875*, pp. 113–115.

(An immature form. See AD. TARGIONI TOZZETTI, *Bull. Soc. Entomol. Italiana*, IV. pp. 84–96, Tav. I. *1872*.)

Giard, Alfred.

Contributions à l'Histoire Naturelle des Synascidies. *Arch. Zool. Expér.*, II. pp. 481–514. *1873*.

(Nauplius of *Ophioseides apoda*, Pl. XIX. fig. 2.)

Sur les Cirripèdes Rhizocéphales. *Comptes Rendus de l'Acad. des Sci., Paris*, Vol. LXXVII. pp. 945–948. *1873*.

Sur l'Embryogénie des Rhizocéphales. *Comptes Rendus de l'Acad. des Sci., Paris*, Vol. LXXIX. pp. 44–46. *1874*.
Trans. in *Ann. Mag. Nat. Hist.* [4], XIV. pp. 381–383. *1874*.

Sur les Isopodes parasites du Genre *Entoniscus*. *Comptes Rendus de l'Acad. des Sci., Paris*, Vol. LXXXVII. pp. 299–301. *1878*.
Trans. in *Ann. Mag. Nat. Hist.* [5], II. pp. 346–348. *1878*.

("Nauplius-eye" in embryo.)

Notes pour servir à l'Histoire du Genre *Entoniscus*. *Journ. de l'Anat. et de la Physiol. (Robin et Pouchet's)*, XIV. pp. 675–700, Pl. XLVI. *1878*.
Trans. by W. S. DALLAS in *Ann. Mag. Nat. Hist.* [5], IV. pp. 137–156, Pl. X. *1879*.

(Development, pp. 693–698. On the eye of *Cypris*-larva of *Cirripedia*, p. 695, foot-note.)

On the Nauplius and Pupa Stage of *Suctoria*. *Ann. Mag. Nat. Hist.* [5], II. pp. 233, 234. Sept. *1878*.

(Fritz Müller's "*Peneus*-nauplius" *not* a larval Suctorian.)

Gissler, Charles F.

Contributions to the Fauna of the New York Croton Water. Microscopical Observations during the Years 1870–71. New York, *1872*. 23 pp., 5 pl.

(Young of *Cyclops* and *Cypris*.)

Goodsir, Henry D. S.

On a New Genus, and on Six New Species of Crustacea, with Observations on the Development of the Egg, and on the Metamorphoses of *Caligus, Carcinus,* and *Pagurus.* *Edinburgh New Philosoph. Journ.*, XXXIII. pp. 174–192, Pl. II., III. *1842.*

The section on development of *Caligus* trans. in *Ann. Sci. Nat.* [2], Zool., XVIII. pp. 181–184. *1842.*

On the Sexes, Organs of Reproduction, and Mode of Development, of the Cirripeds. Account of the Maidre of the Fishermen, and Descriptions of some New Species of Crustaceans. *Edinburgh New Philosoph. Journ.*, XXXV. pp. 88–104, 336–339, Pl. III., IV., VI. *1843.* *Froriep's Neue Notizen,* XXX. col. 193–200, 209–215. *1844.*

Gosse, Philip Henry.

A Naturalist's Rambles on the Devonshire Coast. London, *1853.* xvi. + 451 pp., 28 pl.

(Young of *Hyperia* [?], p. 368, Pl. XXII. fig. 15.)

Tenby: a Sea-side Holiday. London, *1856.* xx. + 400 pp., 24 pl.

(Development of *Balanus*, pp. 115–118, Pl. III., IV. Last zoëa stage and first megalopa stage of *Galatea* [*Porcellana* ?], pp. 169–172, Pl. VII., VIII.; also brief notice in *A Year at the Shore*, p. 194, London, *1865*.)

Gray [J. E.].

Reproduction of *Cirrhipeda.* *Proc. Zoölog. Soc. London*, Pt. 1. pp. 115, 116. *1833.*

(*Balanus Cranchii*.)

Grobben, Carl.

Die Entwickelungsgeschichte der *Moina rectirostris.* Zugleich ein Beitrag zur Kenntniss der Anatomie der Phyllopoden. *Arbeiten aus d. zoolog. Inst. d. Universität Wien u. d. zoolog. Station in Triest*, II. pp. 203–268, Taf. XI.–XVII. *1879.*

Abstr. by P. MAYER in *Zoolog. Jahresber.* 1879, I. pp. 395, 399–401, *1880;* in English, by J. S. KINGSLEY, in *Amer. Naturalist*, XIV. pp. 114–116, 7 figs., February, *1880.*

(Also contains observations on larva of *Cyclops* and *Ergasilus*.)

Die Entwicklungsgeschichte von *Cetochilus septentrionalis* Goodsir. *Arbeiten aus d. zoolog. Inst. d. Universität Wien u. d. zoolog. Station in Triest,* III. pp. 243–282, Taf. XIX.–XXII., 2 cuts. *1881.*

Abstr. in *Journ. Roy. Microscop. Soc.* [2], I. pp. 734–736. *1881.*

(Also contains observations on the formation of the mesoderm in *Phyllopoda* and *Cirripedia.* pp. 29–31.)

Grube, Adolph Eduard.

Bemerkungen über die Phyllopoden, nebst einer Uebersicht ihrer Gattungen und Arten. *Arch. f. Naturgesch.*, *1853*, 1, pp. 71–172, Taf. V.–VIII.

(Observations on development, *passim*.)

Guérin-Méneville, Felix Eduard.

*In RAMON DE LA SAGRA's *Historia Fisica, Politica, y Natural de la Isla de Cuba*. *II. Parte, Historia Natural*, VII. p. xx. ff., Tab. III. Paris, *1856*.

Guilding, L.

Desultory Remarks relative to Points in the Economy of various Crustacea. *Mag. Nat. Hist. (London's)*, VIII. pp. 276, 277. May, *1835*.

(Young of "mountain crab" [?] "leave the egg *perfect*.")

Cf. BELL's *Hist. Brit. Stalk-eyed Crustacea*, Introd., p. xliv. London, *1853*.

Haeckel, Ernst.

Die Gastrula und die Eifurchung der Thiere. *Jenaische Zeitschr.*, IX. ([2], II.) pp. 402–508, Taf. XIX.–XXV. *1875*.

(*Peneus*, pp. 447–452, Taf. XXIII.)

Hailstone, S.

An Illustrated Description of a Species of *Eurynome*, supposed to be hitherto undescribed ; and Notices of some Instances of some Change of Form which occurs in certain cited Species of Crustaceous Animals. *Mag. Nat. Hist. (London's)*, VIII. pp. 549–551. October, *1835*.

Hailstone (S.) and Westwood (J. O.).

Descriptions of some Species of Crustaceous Animals, by S. HAILSTONE, Jr., Esq.: with Illustrations and Remarks, by J. O. WESTWOOD, Esq., F.L.S., etc. *Mag. Nat. Hist. (London's)*, VIII. pp. 261–276. May, *1835*.

(Young of several *Decapoda*.)

Hartmann, Robert.

Beiträge zur anatomische Kenntniss der Schmarotzer-Krebse. 2. *Lernaeocera Barnimii* Mihi. *Arch. f. Anat., Physiol. u. wissensch. Med.*, *1870*, pp. 726–752, Taf. XVII., XVIII.

(Development, p. 749, Taf. XVIII. figs. 21-28.)

Hartog, Marcus. See Addendum, p. 244.

Haswell, William A.

Note on the Phyllosoma Stage of *Ibacus Peronii* Leach. *Proc. Linn. Soc. New South Wales*, IV. pp. 280–282. *1879*.

Henneguy, L. F.

Note sur l'Existence de Globules polaires dans l'Œuf des Crustacés. *Bull. Soc. Philomath., Paris* [7], IV. p. 135, 10 April, *1880*. Trans. in *Ann. Mag. Nat. Hist.* [5], VI. p. 465. December, *1880*.

(Seen in ovum of *Asellus aquaticus*.)

Hensen, V.

Studien über das Gehörorgan der Decapoden. *Zeitschr. f. wissensch. Zool.*, XIII. pp. 319–412, Taf. XIX.–XXII. *1863*.

(Auditory apparatus of zoëa of *Carcinus Mænas*, pp. 340, 362, Taf. XX. fig. 25.)

Herrick, C. L.

Microscopic *Entomostraca. Geolog. & Nat. Hist. Survey of Minnesota, 7th Ann. Rep. for the Year* 1878, pp. 81–123, Pl. I.–XXI. *1879.*
(Nauplii, *passim.*)

Hesse, Eugène.

Mémoire sur les Pranizes et les Ancées. *Ann. Sci. Nat.* [4], Zool., IX. pp. 93–119. *1858.*

Complete memoir in *Mém. prés. par divers Savants à l'Inst. Impér. de France,* XVIII. *1864.*

Mémoire sur les Moyens à l'Aide desquels certains Crustacés Parasites assurent la Conservation de leur Espèce. *Ann. Sci. Nat.* [4], Zool., IX. pp. 120–125, *1858. Comptes Rendus de l'Acad. des Sci., Paris,* XLVI. pp. 1054, 1055, *1858.*
(Parasitic *Copepoda.*)

Complete memoir in *Mém. prés. par divers Savants à l'Inst. Impér. de France,* XVIII. *1864.*

Mémoire sur les Métamorphoses que subissent pendant la Période Embryonnaire les Anatifes appelés Scalpels Obliques. *Ann. Sci. Nat.* [4], Zool., XI. pp. 160–178, *1859.* Short Notice in *Comptes Rendus de l'Acad. des Sci., Paris,* XLVIII. p. 911. *1859.*
(See later paper in *Revue des Sci. Nat.*)

Mémoire sur deux nouveaux Genres de l'Ordre des Crustacés Isopodes Sedentaires et sur les Espèces Types de ces Genres. *Ann. Sci. Nat.* [4], Zool., XV. pp. 91–116, Pl. VIII., IX. *1861.*
(Development of *Athelgue,* pp. 100–102, Pl. VIII. figs. 2^h–2^k.)

Observations sur des Crustacés rares ou nouveaux des Côtes de France. 1er Art. Du Coiliacole sétigère (Nobis), *Coiliacola setigera. Ann. Sci. Nat.* [4], Zool., XVIII. pp. 343–355, Pl. XVIII. *1862.*
(Few observations on development.)

Recherches sur quelques Crustacés rares ou nouveaux des Côtes de France. 2e Mémoire. De la Lernée branchiale et de celle qui vit sur le Gade barbu. 3e Mémoire. Famille des Lernéogastriens, Nobis. Genre Naobranchie, Nobis. *Ann. Sci. Nat.* [4], Zool., XX. pp. 101–132, Pl. I. *1863.*

Mémoire sur les Pranizes et les Ancées et sur les Moyens curieux à l'Aide desquels certains Crustacés Parasites assurent la Conservation de leur Espèce. *Mém. prés. par divers Savants à l'Inst. Impér. de France,* XVIII. *1864.* 74 pp., 5 pl.
Abstr. in *Ann. Mag. Nat. Hist.* [3], XIV. pp. 405–417. *1864.* (Memoir on the *Pranizæ* and *Ancei.*)
Reviewed by C. SPENCE BATE in *Rec. Zoöl. Lit.,* I. (1864), pp. 296–299. *1865.*
(*Praniza, Anceus,* and parasitic *Copepoda.*)

Observations sur des Crustacés rares ou nouveaux des Côtes de France. 3ᵉ Art. *Ann. Sci. Nat.* [5], Zool., I. pp. 333–358, Pl. XI., XII. *1864.*

(Embryos of some species parasitic in Ascidians.)

Mémoire sur des Crustacés rares ou nouveaux des Côtes de France. 4ᵉ Art. Sacculinidés. *Ann. Sci. Nat.* [5], Zool., II. pp. 275–288, Pl. XIX. A. *1864.*

(Includes observations on development.)

Recherches sur les Crustacés rares ou nouveaux des Côtes de France. Complément du 3ᵉ Art. Crustacés parasites vivant dans les Ascidies Phallusiennes. 5ᵉ Art. Genre Pleurocrypte, Nobis. *Ann. Sci. Nat.* [5], Zool., III. pp. 221–242, Pl. IV. *1865.*

Abstr. by W. S. DALLAS in *Ann. Mag. Nat. Hist.* [3], XVI. pp. 162–167. *1865.*

(Young of *Notopterophorus bombyx,* pp. 225, 226 ; *Pleurocrypta Galatea,* pp. 233–235, Pl. IV. figs. 18–28.)

Observations sur des Crustacés rares ou nouveaux des Côtes de France. 6ᵉ Art. *Ann. Sci. Nat.* [5], Zool., IV. pp. 229–258, Pl. VI., VII. *1865.*

(Young of several species found parasitic in compound Ascidians.)

Observations sur des Crustacés rares ou nouveaux des Côtes de France. 7ᵉ Art. Mémoire sur un nouveau Crustacé parasite appartenant à l'Ordre des Lernéidiens, formant la Famille des Lernéosiphonicus et le Genre Leposphile. *Ann. Sci. Nat.* [5], Zool., V. pp. 265–279, Pl. IX. *1866.*

Trans. by W. S. DALLAS in *Ann. Mag. Nat. Hist.* [3], XVIII. pp. 73–82. *1866.*

(Larva, pp. 269, 270, figs. 23–26.)

Observations sur des Crustacés rares ou nouveaux des Côtes de France. 9ᵉ Art. Recherches sur les Genres Doropygus et Dyspontius de M. Thorell. Description de quatre nouveaux Genres: Gastrode, Cheratrichode, Ophthalmopache et Platydurax (Nobis). *Ann. Sci. Nat.* [5], Zool., VI. pp. 51–87, Pl. IV. *1866.*

(Young of *Doropygus,* a parasite of Ascidians, pp. 57, 65.)

Observations sur des Crustacés rares ou nouveaux des Côtes de France. 10ᵉ Art. Peltogastres et Sacculinidiens. *Ann. Sci. Nat.* [5], Zool., VI. pp. 321–360, Pl. XI., XII. *1866.*

(Includes observations on development.)

Observations sur des Crustacés rares ou nouveaux des Côtes de France. 11ᵉ Art. Mémoire concernant deux Crustacés nouveaux trouvés parmi des Ballanes sillonées (*Balanus sulcatus*) et des Anatifes lisses (*Anatifa lævis*). *Ann. Sci. Nat.* [5], Zool., VII. pp. 123–152, Pl. II., III. *1867.*

(Includes observations on larvæ of *Cirripedia.*)

Observations sur des Crustacés rares ou nouveaux des Côtes de France. 14ᵉ Art. Description de deux Sacculinidiens, d'un Peltogastre, d'un Polychliniophile et de deux Cryptopodes nouveaux. *Ann. Sci. Nat.* [5], Zool., VIII. pp. 377–381, *1867;* IX. pp. 53–61, *1868.*

Observations sur des Crustacés rares ou nouveaux des Côtes de France. 15ᵉ Art. Description d'un nouveau Crustacé appartenant au Genre Limnorie. *Ann. Sci. Nat.* [5], Zool., X. pp. 101-120, Pl. IX. *1868.*

(Young, pp. 108, 109, figs. 4, 5.)

Observations sur des Crustacés rares ou nouveaux des Côtes de France. 16ᵉ Art. *Ann. Sci. Nat.* [5], Zool., X. pp. 347-371, Pl. XIX. *1868.*

(Embryo of *Cuma terginigra,* pp. 353, 354, fig. 19.)

Observations sur des Crustacés rares ou nouveaux des Côtes de France. 17ᵉ Art. Description d'un nouveau Crustacé Type d'une nouvelle Famille des Anuelidicoles ; du Genre des Chelonidiformis ; du nouveau Genre Aplopode et de plusieurs autres Crustacés, encore inédits, appartenant aux Genres Polychliniophile, Cryptopode, Botryllophile, Bothacus, Adranesius, Lygephile et Doropygus. *Ann. Sci. Nat.* [5], Zool., XI. pp. 275-308. *1869.*

(Observations on young, *passim.*)

Observations sur des Crustacés rares ou nouveaux des Côtes de France. 18ᵉ Art. Description d'une nouvelle Espèce de Crustacé parasite des l'Ordre des Lernéidiens de la Famille des Lernéocericus, et du Genre Leruée : Lernée du Gade-petit, *Lernæa Gadni minutus* [*Gadi minuti*] (Nobis). *Ann. Sci. Nat.* [5], Zool., XIII., Art. 4. 30 pp., Pl. I. *1870.*

(Embryology, pp. 7-15, Pl. I.)

Mémoire sur des Crustacés rares ou nouveaux des Côtes de France. 21ᵉ [20ᵉ] Art. Mémoire sur la Famille des Sphéromiens, à l'Occasion des Affinités et des Relations sexuelles qui paraissent exister entre les Sphéromiens et les Cymodocéens d'une part, et les Dynaméniens et les Néséens d'autre part. *Ann. Sci. Nat.* [5], Zool., XVII., Art. 1. 35 pp., Pl. I.-III. *1873.*

(Treats of young, *passim.*)

Mémoire sur des Crustacés rares ou nouveaux des Côtes de France. 21ᵉ Art. Description de Crustacés nouveaux appartenant à la Légion des Edriophthalmes, de l'Ordre des Amphipodes, de la Famille des Piscicoles, de la Tribu des Enoplopodes, Nobis, du Genre des Ichthyomyzoques, Nobis. *Ann. Sci. Nat.* [5], Zool., XVII., Art. 7. 16 pp., Pl. IV. *1873.*

(Young of *Ichthyomyzocus Lophii* resembles adult, p. 11.)

Observations biologiques concernant les Cymothoadiens parasites et notamment le Cymothoé Œstre, *Cymothoa Œstrum. Revue des Sci. Nat.*, II. pp. 1-13. June, *1873.*

(Remarks on the young.)

Mémoire sur des Crustacés rares ou nouveaux des Côtes de France. 23ᵉ Art. Pranizes et Ancées nouveaux. *Ann. Sci. Nat.* [5], Zool., XIX., Art. 8. 29 pp., Pl. XXI., XXII. *1874.*

Description des Crustacés rares ou nouveaux des Côtes de France. 25ᵉ Art. Description du *Pagurus misanthropus;* son Ontogénie, sa Physiologie et sa Biologie. — Description d'un Larve trouvée mêlée à celles de ce Crustacé. — Observations concernant les *Pagurus Ulidianus* et *Prideauxii. Ann. Sci. Nat.* [6], Zool., III., Art. 5.   42 pp. Pl. V., VI. *1876.*

Description des Crustacés rares ou nouveaux des Côtes de France. 26ᵉ Art. Nouvelles Observations sur les Métamorphoses embryonnaires des Crustacés de l'Ordre des Isopodes sedentaires. — Description de trois nouvelles Espèces de ces Crustacés, dont deux appartiennent au Genre Athelgue et l'autre au Genre Pleurocrypte. *Ann. Sci. Nat.* [6], Zool., IV., Art. 2.   48 pp., Pl. VII.–IX. *1876.*

Description de la Série complète des Métamorphoses que subissent, durant la Période embryonnaire, les Anatifes désignés sous le Nom de Scalpel oblique ou de Scalpel vulgaire. *Revue des Sci. Nat.* [after 1874].   31 pp., 2 pl.

Description d'un nouvel Ancée, l'Ancée du Congre, *Anceus Congeri,* faite sur des Individus vivants.   25 pp., 1 pl.   Ex. de la *Revue des Sci. Nat.,* IV.   Mars, *1876.*

(Includes young or *Praniza* state.)

Remarques sur le Genre Chalime.   *Ann. Sci. Nat.* [6], Zool., V., Art. 10. 3 pp. *1877.*

(This so-called genus is a larva.)

Description des Mâles, non encore connus, des Lernanthropes de Gisler et de Kroyer, ainsi que de la Femelle d'une Espèce nouvelle, dessinés et peints d'après des Individus vivants.   30 pp., 3 pl.   Ex. de la *Revue des Sci. Nat.,* VI., déc., *1877 ;* VII., juin, *1878.*

Description des Crustacés rares ou nouveaux des Côtes de France décrits et peints sur des Individus vivants.   29ᵉ Art. Description de dix nouveaux Crustacés, dont sept appartiennent du Genre *Cycnus* de Kroyer et trois au Genre *Kroyeria* de Van Beneden, tous décrits et dessinés sur des Individus vivants. *Ann. Sci. Nat.* [6], Zool., VIII., Art. 11.   34 pp., Pl. XIX.–XXI. *1879.*

(Larva of *Kroyeria,* a parasitic Copepod, Pl. XXI. fig. 10.)

Description des Crustacés rares ou nouveaux des Côtes de France décrits sur des Individus vivants.   30ᵉ Art. Description d'un nouveau Crustacé parasite appartenant à la Sous-Classe des Crustacés suceurs, de l'Ordre des Lernéides, formant la nouvelle Famille des Lernéopalmiens et le nouveau Genre des *Stylophores,* décrits et dessiné d'après des Individus vivants. *Ann. Sci. Nat.* [6], Zool., VIII., Art. 15.   16 pp., Pl. XXVIII. *1879.*

(Young of *Stylophorus hippocephalus,* p. 6, figs. 22-25.)

Hoek, P. P. C.

*Eerste Bijdrage tot een nauwkeuriger Kennis der Sessile Cirripedien. *1875.* 94 pp., 2 pl. (Inaugural Dissertation.)

Zur Entwickelungsgeschichte der Entomostraken.   I. Embryologie von *Balanus. Niederländisches Arch. f. Zool.*, III. pp. 47–82, Taf. III., IV. *1876.*

Zur Entwickelungsgeschichte der Entomostraken.   II. Zur Embryologie der freilebenden Copepoden. *Niederländisches Arch. f. Zool.*, IV. pp. 55–74, Taf. V., VI. *1877.*

Hosius, A.

Ueber die *Gammarus*-Arten der Gegend von Bonn.   *Arch. f. Naturgesch. 1850*, 1, pp. 233–248, Taf. III., IV.

(Young, pp. 243 *et seq.*, figs. 23, 24.)

Huxley, Thomas H.

Lectures on General Natural History.   Lecture XI.   *The Medical Times and Gazette*, new ser., XIV. pp. 638, 639, fig. 1.   June 27, *1857.*

Also in *Trans. Linn. Soc. London*, XXII., Pt. III., *1858* (see next title), and *A Manual of the Anatomy of Invertebrated Animals*, pp. 350–355, fig. 79, London, *1877.*

(Development of *Mysis.*)

On the Agamic Reproduction and Morphology of *Aphis*, Pt. II.   § 2. Embryogeny of *Mysis*, as exemplifying the *Crustacea*.   § 3. Embryogeny of *Scorpio*, as exemplifying the *Arachnida*.   § 4. Generalizations regarding the Embryogeny of the *Articulata*, and Morphological Laws based on them.   § 5. The Embryogeny of *Articulata*, *Mollusca*, and *Vertebrata* compared.   *Trans. Linn. Soc. London*, XXII., Pt. III. pp. 225–234. *1858.*

The Crayfish.   An Introduction to the Study of Zoölogy.   London and New York, *1880.*   371 pp., 81 cuts.

(Development, pp. 39–44, 205–226, figs. 8, 57–60.)

Joly, N.

Histoire d'un petit Crustacé (*Artemia salina* Leach), auquel on a faussement attribué la Coloration en Rouge des Marais salants Méditerranéens, suivie de Recherches sur la Cause réelle de cette Coloration. *Ann. Sci. Nat.* [2], Zool., XIII. pp. 225–290, Pl. VII., VIII. *1840.*

(Development, pp. 257–262, Pl. VII.)

Also printed with the same title at Montpellier, *1840.*   72 pp., 3 pl.

Recherches Zoologiques, Anatomiques et Physiologiques sur l'*Isaura cycladoïdes*, nouveau Genre de Crustacé à Test bivalve, découvert aux Environs de Toulouse. *Ann. Sci. Nat.* [2], Zool., XVII. pp. 293–349, Pl. VII.–IX. A. *1842.*

(*Estheria.*   Development, pp. 321–330, Pl. IX. A.)

Sur les Métamorphoses d'un Crustacé de la Tribu des Salicoques, trouvé dans le Canal du Midi. *Comptes Rendus de l'Acad. des Sci., Paris*, XV. pp. 36, 37. *1842*.

(*Caridina Desmarestii*.)

Études sur les Mœurs, la Développement et les Métamorphoses d'une petite Salicoque d'Eau douce (*Caridina Desmarestii*), suivies de quelques Réflexions sur les Métamorphoses des Crustacés Décapodes en général. *Ann. Sci. Nat.* [2], XIX. pp. 34-86, Pl. III., IV. *1843*.

Also published under the following title : —

Recherches sur le Développement et les Métamorphoses d'une petite Salicoque d'Eau douce (*Caridina Desmarestii* Nobis, *Hippolyte Desmarestii* Millet), suivies de quelques Réflexions sur les Métamorphoses des Crustacés Décapodes en général. Toulouse, *1843*. 59 pp., 2 pl.

Jurine, Louis.

Mémoire sur l'Argule foliacé (*Argulus foliaceus*). *Ann. du Mus. d'Hist. Nat.*, VII. pp. 431-458, Pl. XXVI. *1806*.

(Development, pp. 452-456.)

Histoire des Monocles qui se trouvent aux Euvirons de Genève. Genève, *1820*. 258 pp., 22 pl.

(Young of *Copepoda, Cladocera, Ostracoda, passim*.)

Translation of the Memoir of SCHÄFFER, Sur les Monocles à queue, ou Puces d'Eau rameuses, pp. 181-197.

(Development, pp. 196, 197.)

Mémoire sur le Chirocéphale. Par BÉNÉDICT PREVOST, pp. 201-244, Pl. XX.-XXII.

(Development, pp. 214-220.)

Kellicott, D. S.

A Larval Argulus. *The North American Entomologist*, I. pp. 57-60, Feb. *1880*.

Kinahan [John Robert].

Notes on the foregoing Paper [Melville's Carcinological Notes], with a Supplement to his List of Dublin Crustacea. **Proc. Dublin Nat. Hist. Soc.*, II. pp. 43-51. *1856-59*. *Nat. Hist. Rev.*, IV. Proc. Soc., pp. 153-162. *1857*.

(Zoëa of *Pirimela denticulata*, pp. 156, 157, Pl. IX. figs. 4-6.)

Remarks on the Zoë of *Eurynome aspera*, and the Habits of the Animal in Confinement. **Proc. Dublin Nat. Hist. Soc.*, 4 Dec. *1857*. **Nat. Hist. Rev.*, V. Proc. Soc., pp. 37-39, *1858*. *Ann. Mag. Nat. Hist.*, [3], I. pp. 233-235. *1858*.

Kollar, Vincenz.

Beiträge zur Kenntniss der Lernaeenartigen Crustaceen. *Annalen des Wiener Museums der Naturgeschichte*, I. pp. 79-92, Taf. IX., X. *1836*.

(Development of *Basanistes Huchonis*, pp. 87-90, Taf. X.)

Koren (J.) and Danielssen (D.).

Bidrag til Cirripedernes Udvikling. *Nyt Mag. Naturvid.*, V. pp. 262–264, Tab. II. figs. 1–3. *1848. Isis, 1848*, col. 204, 205, Taf. II. figs. 11–13.

(*Alepas squalicola.*)

Kossman, Robby.

Beiträge zur Anatomie der schmarotzenden Rankenfüssler. *Arbeit. aus dem zoolog.-zootom. Inst. in Würzburg*, I. pp. 97–137, Taf. V.–VII. *1872. Verhandl. d. physikal.-medicin. Gesell. in Würzburg* [2], III. pp. 296–335, Taf. XVI.–XVIII. *1872.*

(Development, pp. 115–118, Taf. VII. 1–6.)

Suctoria und *Lepadidae.* Untersuchungen über die durch Parasitismus hervorgerufenen Umbildungen in der Familie der *Pedunculata. Arbeit. aus dem zoolog.-zootom. Inst. in Würzburg*, I. pp. 179–207, Taf. X. *1872–74. Verhandl. d. physikal.-medicin. Gesell. in Würzburg* [2], V. pp. 129–157, Taf. I., II. *1873.*

(Development, pp. 195–200, Taf. X., XI.)

Studien über Bopyriden. II. *Bopyrina Virbii;* Beiträge zur Kenntniss der Anatomie und Metamorphose der Bopyriden. *Zeitschr. f. wissensch. Zool.*, XXXV. pp. 666–680, Taf. XXXIV., XXXV. *1881.*

Kröyer, Henrik.

Bopyrus abdominalis. Naturhistorisk Tidsskr., III. pp. 102–112, 289–299, Taf. I., II. *1840. Isis, 1841*, col. 693–698, 707–713, Taf. II., III.

Trans. by LEREBOULLET in *Ann. Sci. Nat.* [2], Zool., XVII. pp. 142–152, Pl. VI. *1842.*

(Contains observations on development.)

Monografisk Fremstilling af Slægten Hippolyte's nordiske Arter. Med Bidrag til Dekapodernes Udviklingshistorie. *K. Danske Vidensk. Selsk. naturvid. og mathem. Afh.*, IX. pp. 209–360, 6 pl. *1842.*

(Larval stages of *Hippolyte*, *Homarus*, and *Cymopolia*, pp. 245–262, Pl. V. figs. 111–119, VI.)

In GAIMARD's *Voyages de la Commission Scientifique du Nord en Scandinavie, en Laponie au Spitzberg et aux Feröe pendant les Années* 1838, 1839 *et* 1840, *sur la Corvette la Recherche.* Paris, *1842–45.* Zoologie. Crustacés.

(Young *Caridea*, Pl. VII.; *Mysis*, Pl. IX.; *Bopyrus*, Pl. XXVIII.; *Pycnogonida*, Pl. XXXIX.)

[On the Development of *Peltogaster* and *Sylon.*] *Overs. K. Danske Vidensk. Selsk. Forhandl. 1855.* Nr. 4, p. 130.

Trans. by CREPLIN in *Zeitschr. gesammt. Naturwissen.*, VIII. pp. 421, 422. *1856.*

Bidrag til Kundskab om Snyltekrebsene. *Naturhistorisk Tidsskr.* [3], II. pp. 75–426, Tab. I.–XVIII. *1863–64.*

(Larva of *Lesteira Lumpi*, Tab. XVIII. figs. 5 f, 5 g. *1864.*)

Krohn, August.

Beobachtungen über die Entwickelung der Cirripedien. *Arch. f. Naturgesch.*, *1860*, 1, pp. 1–8, Taf. 1. figs. 1–3.

Trans. by W. S. Dallas in *Ann. Mag. Nat. Hist.* [3], VI. pp. 423–428, Pl. VII. figs. 1–3. *1860*.

Lacaze-Duthiers, Henri de.

Mémoire sur un Mode nouveau de Parasitisme observé sur un Animal non décrit. *Comptes Rendus de l'Acad. des Sci., Paris*, LXI. pp. 838–841. *1865*.

Abstr. in *Ann. Mag. Nat. Hist.* [3], XVII. pp. 155, 156. Feb., *1866*.

(*Laura Gerardiæ*. Development, p. 841.)

Histoire de la *Laura Gerardiæ*, Type nouveau de Crustacé parasite. *Archives de Zool. Expér.*, VIII. pp. 537–581. *1879–80*. 7 cuts.

Ex. from *Mém. Acad. Sci.*, where it appears *in extenso*, with 8 plates.

(Parasitic Cirriped. Development, pp. 575–577, fig. 7.)

Lang, Arnold.

*Ueber die Metamorphose der Naupliuslarven von *Balanus* mit Rücksicht auf die Gestaltung der Gliedmassen und die Verwandlung in die *Cypris*-ähnliche Larve. *Mitth. aarg. nat. Gesell.*, I. pp. 104–115, 1 Taf. *1878*.

Die Dotterfurchung von *Balanus*. *Jenaische Zeitschr.*, XII. ([2], V.), pp. 671–674, Taf. XX., XXI. *1878*.

Latreille [P. A.].

In Cuvier's *Règne Animal*. Paris.

(Young *Isopoda* at birth like parent form, 1st ed., III. p. 50, *1817*. So also with *Astacus*, 2d ed., IV. p. 90, *1829*. Young stage of *Squilla* made a genus under the name *Erichthus*, 1st ed., III. p. 43, *1817*.)

La Valette St. George, Adolphe de.

Ueber die Entwicklungs-Geschichte der Amphipoden. *Sitzungsber. Niederrhein. Gesell. f. Natur- u. Heilkunde zu Bonn*, XVI. pp. 94–98. *1859*.

Studien über die Entwickelung der Amphipoden. *Abh. d. naturfor. Gesell. Halle*, V. pp. 153–166, 2 pl. *1860*.

Ueber die Entwickelung der Isopoden. *Amtlicher Bericht über die 39 Versamml. Deutsch. Naturforsch. u. Aerzte zu Giessen*, 1864, p. 168. *1865*.

Leach, William Elford.

Malacostraca Podophthalmata Britanniæ; or Descriptions of such British Species of the Linnean Genus *Cancer* as have their Eyes elevated on Footstalks. London, *1815*. 44 pl.

(Genus *Megalopa* founded upon young stage of *Brachyura*, Pl. XVI.)

In *Journ. de Physique, 1818*, and *Appendix to Tuckey's Expedition to explore the Source of the River Zaire*, London, *1818* (see *Isis*, 1818, col. 2083–2086), Leach founded the genera *Phyllosoma, Alima, Smerdis, &c.*, for the reception of what are now known to be larval stages of Crustacea.

For the various systematic works on zoölogy in which the many so-called species of these and other genera established upon young stages have been described, see MILNE EDWARDS, *Hist. Nat. Crust.*, II.; F. C. LUKIS, *Mag. Nat. Hist.*, VIII. p. 461, &c.

Lereboullet, A.

Résumé d'un Travail d'Embryologie Comparée sur le Développement du Brochet, de la Perche et de l'Écrevisse. Suite Deuxième Partie. Embryologie de l'Écrevisse. *Ann. Sci. Nat.* [4], Zool., II. pp. 39–50. *1854.*

Recherches d'Embryologie Comparée sur le Développement du Brochet, de la Perche et de l'Écrevisse. *Mém. prés. par divers Savants étrangers à l'Acad. des Sci. de l'Inst. Impér. de France*, XVII. pp. 447–805, 6 pl. *1862.*

(*Astacus*, pp. 650–768, Pl. IV.–VI.)

Observations sur la Génération et le Développement de la Limnadie de Hermann (*Limnadia Hermanni* Ad. Brongn.). *Ann. Sci. Nat.* [5], Zool., V. pp. 283–308, Pl. XII. *1866.*

Leuckart, Rudolph.

Carcinologisches. Einige Bemerkungen über *Sacculina* Thomps. (*Pachybdella* Dies., *Peltogaster* Rathke, p. p.). *Arch. f. Naturgesch.* 1859, 1, pp. 232–241, Taf. VI.

(Embryo, p. 239.)

Trans. by W. S. DALLAS in *Ann. Mag. Nat. Hist.* [3], IV. pp. 422–429, Pl. VII. *1859.*

(Embryo, p. 428.)

See also **Frey, Heinrich.**

Leydig, Franz.

Ueber *Argulus foliaceus.* Ein Beitrag zur Anatomie, Histologie, und Entwicklungsgeschichte dieses Thieres. *Zeitschr. f. wissensch. Zool.*, II. pp. 323–349, Taf. XIX., XX. *1850.*

(Development, pp. 344–347, Taf. XX. fig. 8.)

Ueber *Artemia salina* und *Branchipus stagnalis.* Beitrag zur anatomischen Kenntniss dieser Thiere. *Zeitschr. f. wissensch. Zool.*, III. pp. 280–307, Taf. VIII. *1851.*

(Development, pp. 304–306.)

Naturgeschichte der Daphniden (*Crustacea Cladocera*). Tübingen, *1860.* 252 pp., 10 pl.

(Reproduction, pp. 58–75.)

Reviewed by J. LUBBOCK in *Nat. Hist. Rev.*, *1861*, pp. 22–33.

Liljeborg, Wilh.

Norges Crustaceer. *Öfvers. K. Svenska Vetensk.-Akad. Förhandl.*, VIII. (1851), pp. 19–25. *1852.*

(Young of *Hyas. Zoëa pelagica* Bosc the young of *Hyas?* pp. 20, 21, 25.)

De Crustaceis ex Ordinibus Tribus: Cladocera, Ostracoda et Copepoda, in Scania occurrentibus. Om de inom Skåne förekommande Crustaceer af ordningarne *Cladocera, Ostracoda* och *Copepoda.* Lund, *1853.* 222 pp., 26 pl.

(Young *Canthocamptus,* pp. 148, 149, Pl. XVI. fig. 6; *Cyclops,* pp. 156–158, Pl. XXVI. fig. 19.)

Les Genres *Liriope* et *Peltogaster* II. Rathke. *Nova Acta Reg. Soc. Scient. Upsal.* [3], III. pp. 1–35, Pl. I.–III. *1859.* (**Arsskr.,* I. pp. 137–147. *1860.*)

Abstr. in English in *Ann. Mag. Nat. Hist.* [3], VI. pp. 162–173, 260–267, Pl. IV. *1860.*

(Includes development.)

Supplément au Mémoire sur les Genres *Liriope* et *Peltogaster* II. Rathke. *Nova Acta Reg. Soc. Scient. Upsal.* [3], III. pp. 73–102, Pl. VI.–IX. *1860.*

Abstr. in *Ann. Mag. Nat. Hist.* [3], VII. pp. 47–63, Pl. II., III. *1861.* *Ann. Sci. Nat.* [5], Zool., 11. pp. 289–355, Pl. XX. *1864.*

(Includes development.)

Liriope och *Peltogaster* II. Rathke. *Öfvers. K. Svenska Vetensk.-Akad. Förhandl.,* XVI. (1859), pp. 213–217. *1860. Forhandl. Skand. Natur-forsk.,* VIII. (1860), pp. 677–684. Kiöbenhavn, *1861.*

Beskrifning öfver tvenne märkliga Crustaceer af Ordningen *Cladocera. Öfvers. K. Svenska Vetensk.-Akad. Förhandl.,* XVII. (1860), pp. 265–271, Taf. VII., VIII. *1861.*

Trans. in *Ann. Mag. Nat. Hist.* [3], IX. pp. 132–136, Pl. VIII. *1862.*

(Young *Leptodora hyalina,* p. 267, Taf. VII. fig. 2; *Bythotrephes longimanus,* Taf. VIII. fig. 24.)

Lindström, G.

Om Larven till en Art af Slägtet *Peltogaster. Öfvers. K. Svenska Vetensk.-Akad. Förhandl.* XII. (1855), pp. 361–363, Tab. XIII. B. *1856.*

Lubbock, John.

An Account of the Two Methods of Reproduction in *Daphnia,* and of the Structure of the Ephippium. *Phil. Trans. Roy. Soc. London,* CXLVII. pp. 79–100, Pl. VI., VII. *1857.*

Ludwig, Hubert.

Ueber die Eibildung im Thierreiche. *Arbeit. aus dem zoolog.-zootom. Inst. in Würzburg,* 1. pp. 287–510, Taf. XIII.–XV. *1874. Verhandl. d. physikal.-medicin. Gesell. in Würzburg* [2], VII. pp. 33–256, Taf. I.–III. *1874.*

(On the Crustacean egg, pp. 379–401 [125–147], Taf. XIII., XIV. [I., II.].)

Mayer, Paul.

Zur Entwicklungsgeschichte der Dekapoden. *Jenaische Zeitschr.*, XI. ([2], IV.) pp. 188-269, Taf. XIII.–XV. *1877.*

(Embryology of *Eupagurus Prideauxii*, pp. 188-246,Taf. XIII., XIV. Morphology of the caudal fin of the zoëa (*Zur Kenntniss der Zoëa-Gestalt*), pp. 246-262, Taf. XV.)

Abstr. in *Hofmann u. Schwalbe's Jahresber.*, VI. 2e Abt. pp. 160-162. *1878.*

Carcinologische Mittheilungen. III. Ueber einige Jugendstadien von *Penaeus Caramote.* *Mittheil. aus der zoolog. Station zu Neapel*, 1. pp. 49-51. *1878.*

Carcinologische Mittheilungen. VII. Ein neuer parasitischer Copepode. *Mittheil. aus der zoolog. Station zu Neapel*, I. pp. 515-521, Taf. XVII. *1879.*

(*Ive Balanoglossi n. sp.* Nauplius, p. 519, Taf. XVII. figs. 10-12.)

Carcinologische Mittheilungen. IX. Die Metamorphosen von *Palaemonetes varians* Leach. *Mittheil. aus der Zoolog. Station zu Neapel*, II. pp. 197-221, Taf. X. *1880.*

(Includes notice of larva of *Squilla* just hatched from the egg, p. 219.)

Mecznikow. *See* **Metschnikoff.**

Meinert, Fr. *See* **Schiödte, Jörgen C.**

Meissner, Georg.

Beobachtungen über das Eindringen der Samenelemente in den Dotter, Nro. II. *Zeitschr. f. wissensch. Zool.*, VI. pp. 272-295, Taf. IX. *1855.*

(Micropyle in egg of *Gammarus*, pp. 284, 285. 293, 294, fig. 9.)

Méneville. *See* **Guérin-Méneville.**

Metschnikoff, Elias.

Istoriya Razvitiya Nebalia. Sravnitelno-embriologitshesky Otsherk. [History of the Development of *Nebalia*. A Comparative Embryological Essay.] *Zapiski Imp. Akad. Nauk*, XIII., *1868.* [*Mem. Imper. Acad. of Sciences*, XIII. St. Petersburg, *1868.*] 48 pp., 2 pl.

Noticed in *Rec. Zoölog. Lit.*, VI. (1869), p. 617. *1870.*

Ueber ein Larvenstadium von *Euphausia*. *Zeitschr. f. wissensch. Zool.*, XIX. pp. 479-481, Taf. XXXVI. *1869.*

Ueber den Naupliuszustand von *Euphausia*. *Zeitschr. f. wissensch. Zool.*, XXI. pp. 397-401, Taf. XXXIV. *1871.*

Metzger, A.

Ueber das Männchen und Weibchen der Gattung *Lernaea* vor dem Eintritt der sogen. rückschreitenden Metamorphose. *Arch. f. Naturgesch. 1868*, 1, pp. 106-110. *Nachrichten Kön. Gesell. Wissensch. Göttingen, 1868*, pp. 31-36.

Trans. by W. S. DALLAS, *Ann. Mag. Nat. Hist.* [4], III. pp. 154-157. *1869.*

Milne Edwards, Henri.

Description des Genres Glaucothoé, Sicyonie, Sergeste et Acète, de l'Ordre des Crustacés Décapodes. *Ann. Sci. Nat.*, XIX. pp. 333–352, Pl. VIII.–XI. *1830.*

(A young stage of a Pagurid made the type of a new genus, *Glaucothoé*, pp 334–339, Pl. VIII.)

Histoire Naturelle des Crustacés, comprenant l'Anatomie, la Physiologie et la Classification de ces Animaux. Paris, *1834, 1837, 1840.* 3 vols. and Atlas, 1638 pp., 44 pl. (Suites à Buffon.)

(Remarks on development, *passim :* especially Vol. I. pp. 175–200, Vol. II. pp. 260–264 (*Megalops, Monolepis*), pp. 431–438 (*Zoëa*).)

Observations sur les Changements de Forme que divers Crustacés éprouvent dans le jeune Âge. *Ann. Sci. Nat.* [2], Zool., III. pp. 321–334, Pl. XIV. *1835. Arch. f. Naturgesch.*, *1836*, 2, pp. 225–227.

(*Cymothoë, Anilocra, Cyamus, Phronima, Amphithoë, Nazia.*)

Rapport sur un Travail de M. Hesse, relatif aux Métamorphoses des Ancées et des Caliges, fait à l'Académie des Sciences, le 28 Juin 1858. *Ann. Sci. Nat.* [4], Zool., IX. pp. 89–92. *1858. Comptes Rendus de l'Acad. des Sci.*, *Paris*, XLVI. pp. 1256–1259. *1858.*

Montagu, George.

Description of several Marine Animals found on the South Coast of Devonshire. *Trans. Linn. Soc. London*, VII. pp. 61–85, Pl. VI., VII. *1804.* (Read December 7, 1802.)

(" *Cancer rhomboidalis,*" p. 65, Tab. VI. fig. 1, is a megalopa. Observed the young of " *Cancer Phasma* " [*Caprella*] crawl from abdominal pouch of parent, "all perfectly formed," p. 67.)

Müller, Fritz.

Die Rhizocephalen, eine neue Gruppe schmarotzender Kruster. *Arch. f. Naturgesch.*, *1862*, 1, pp. 1–9, Taf. I.

Trans. by W. S. DALLAS in *Ann. Mag. Nat. Hist.* [3], X. pp. 44–50, Pl. II. figs. 1–7. *1862.*

(Describes larva of *Lernæodiscus* and *Sacculina*.)

Entoniscus Porcellanae, eine neue Schmarotzerassel. *Arch. f. Naturgesch.*, *1862*, 1, pp. 10–18, Taf. II.

Trans. by W. S. DALLAS in *Ann. Mag. Nat. Hist.* [3], X. pp. 87–93, Pl. II. figs. 8–16. *1862.*

(Larva described and figured.)

Die Verwandlung der Porcellanen. Vorläufige Mittheilung. *Arch. f. Naturgesch.*, *1862*, 1, pp. 194–199, Taf. VII.

Trans. by W. S. DALLAS in *Ann. Mag. Nat. Hist.* [3], XI. pp. 47–50, Pl. I. *1863.*

Bruchstück zur Entwickelungsgeschichte der Maulfüsser. *Arch. f. Naturgesch.*, XXVIII. pp. 352–361, Taf. XIII. *1862.*

Trans. by W. S. DALLAS in *Ann. Mag. Nat. Hist.* [3], XII. pp. 13–19, Pl. II. *1863.*

Ein zweites Bruchstück aus der Entwickelungsgeschichte der Maulfüsser. *Arch. f. Naturgesch.*, XXIX. pp. 1–7, Taf. I. *1863.*

Die Verwandlung der Garneelen. Erster Beitrag. *Arch. f. Naturgesch.*, XXIX. pp. 8–23, Taf. II. *1863.*

Trans. by W. S. DALLAS in *Ann. Mag. Nat. Hist.* [3], XIV. pp. 104–115, Pl. IV. *1864.*

Reviewed by C. SPENCE BATE in *Rec. Zoölog. Lit.*, I. (1864), pp. 280–285. *1865.*

(*Peneus.*)

Die zweite Entwickelungstufe der Wurzelkrebse (*Rhizocephala*). *Arch. f. Naturgesch.*, XXIX. pp. 24–33, Taf. III. figs. 1–7. *1863.*

Für Darwin. Leipzig. *1864.* 91 pp., 67 cuts.

English transl. by W. S. DALLAS: Facts and Arguments for Darwin. With Additions by the Author. London, *1869.* 144 pp., 67 cuts.

Reviewed by C. SPENCE BATE in *Rec. Zoölog. Lit.*, I. (1864), pp. 261–270. *1865.*

(General work on development of Crustacea, with many original observations.)

Bruchstücke zur Naturgeschichte der Bopyriden. *Jenaische Zeitschr.*, VI. pp. 53–72, Taf. III., IV. *1871.* [*1869 ?*]

(Includes observations on development.)

Ueber die Naupliusbrut der Garneelen. *Zeitschr. f. wissensch. Zool.*, XXX. pp. 163–166. *1878.*

Trans. in *Ann. Mag. Nat. Hist.* [5], I. pp. 481–485. *1878.*

Wasserthiere in Baumwipfeln. *Elpidium Bromeliarum. Kosmos*, VI. pp. 386–388, 15 figs. Feb. *1880.*

Translated with title: An Entomostracon living in Tree-tops, in *Nature*, XXII. pp. 55, 56. May 20, *1880.*

(Egg and young figured. *Ostracoda.*)

Palaemon Potiuna. Ein Beispiel abgekürzter Verwandlung. *Zoolog. Anzeig.*, III. pp. 152–157, April 5, *1880 ;* p. 233, May 10, *1880.*

Die Putzfüsse der Kruster. *Kosmos*, VII. pp. 148–152, 15 figs. May, *1880.*

(*Trichodactylus* leaves the egg in the perfect form, p. 152.)

See also **Bate, C. Spence.**

Müller, Otho Fredericus.

*Entomostraca, seu Insecta testacea quæ in Aquis Daniæ et Norvegiæ reperit, descripsit et Iconibus illustravit. Lipsiæ et Hafniæ, *1785.*

(Many larvæ represented. *Nauplius.* See reproduction of figures in *Encyclopédie Méthodique*, Pl. CCLXIV.–CCLXVIII.)

Zoologia Danica seu Animalium Daniæ et Norvegiæ rariorum ac minus noto-rum Descriptiones et Historia. Hafniæ, *1788, 1789, 1806.* 4 vols., 225 pp., 160 pl.

(Young *Mysis*, II., Tab. LXVI. fig. 9, *1788.* *" Cancer Faeroensis,"* III. p. 56, Tab. CXIV., *1789,* = megalopa.)

Müller, P. E.

Bidrag til Cladocerernes Forplantningshistorie. *Naturhistorisk Tidsskr.* [3], V. pp. 295-354, Tab. XIII. *1868.* *Forhandl. Skand. Naturforsk.*, X. (1868), pp 530-540. *1869.* *Arch. Sci. Phys. Nat.*, XXXVII. pp. 357-372. *1870.*

Noticed by GERSTAECKER in *Arch. f. Naturgesch.*, *1869,* 2, pp. 190-192.

Müller, Wilhelm.

Beitrag zur Kenntniss der Fortpflanzung und der Geschlechtsverhältnisse der Ostracoden nebst Beschreibung einer neuen Species der Gattung *Cypris.* *Zeitschr. gesammt. Naturwissen.* [3], V. pp. 221-246, Taf. IV., V. *1880.*

(On parthenogenesis in *Ostracoda.* First stage of **Cythere lutea**, **Taf. V. fig. 2.**)

Münter (Jul.) and Buchholz (Reinh.).

Ueber Balanus improvisus Darw. var. *gryphicus* Münter. *Mitth. naturwissensch. Vereins v. Neu-Vorpommern. u. Rügen*, I. pp. 1-40, 2 pl. *1869.* *Zeitschr. gesammt. Naturwissen.*, XXXVI. pp. 529, 530. *1870.*

(Contains observations on development.)

Noll, F. C.

Kochlorine hamata N., ein bohrender Cirripede. (Vorläufige Mittheilung.) *Bericht über d. Senckenbergische naturforsch. Gesell. Frankfurt am Main, 1872-73*, pp. 50-58. **Tageblatt d. 46. Versammlung deutsch. Naturforsch. u. Aerzte, Wiesbaden*, p. 131. *1873.*

Kochlorine hamata N., ein bohrendes Cirriped. *Zeitschr. f. wissensch. Zool.*, XXV. pp. 114-128, Taf. VI. 20 Nov. *1874.*

(Larvæ described and figured.)

Nordmann, Alexander v.

Mikrographische Beiträge zur Naturgeschichte der wirbellosen Thiere. Zweites Heft. Berlin, *1832.* xviii. $+$ 150 pp., 10 pl.

(Development of *Ergasilus*, pp. 11-15, Pl. II. figs. 7-9; of *Achtheres*, pp. 76-85, Pl. IV. figs. 5-12; of *Tracheliastes*, p. 99, Pl. VII. figs. 7, 8; of *Lernæocera*, pp. 127-130, Pl. VI. figs. 5-7.)

Neue Beiträge zur Kenntniss parasitischer Copepoden. Erster Beitrag. *Bull. Soc. Impér. des Nat. Moscou*, XXXVII. Pt. II., pp. 461-520, Pl. V.-VIII. *1864.*

(Larvæ of *Lernanthropus Kröyeri*, Pl. VII. figs. 7, 8.)

Olivier [Ant. Gu.].

Encyclopédie Méthodique, Hist. Nat., VI. Paris, *1791.*

(Observations on young *Gammarus*, p. 183.)

Packard, A. S., Jr.

Life Histories of the Crustacea and Insects. *Amer. Naturalist*, IX. pp. 583–622. Nov. *1875.*

(General account of the development of Crustacea, pp. 583–605. Original observations on development of *Gelasimus pugnax*, p. 603.)

Appears also in the author's *Life Histories of Animals including Man or Outlines of Comparative Embryology*, pp. 167–189. New York, *1876.*

Notes on the Early Larval Stages of the Fiddler Crab, and of *Alpheus. Amer. Naturalist*, XV. pp. 784–789, figs. Oct. *1881.*

(*Gelasimus pugnax, Alpheus heterochelis.*)

Pagenstecher, H. Alex.

Untersuchungen über niedere Seethiere aus Cette. II. Abtheilung. IX. Beitrag zur Anatomie und Entwickelungsgeschichte von *Lepas pectinata. Zeitschr. f. wissensch. Zool.*, XIII. pp. 86–106, Taf. V., VI. *1863.*

Panceri, Paolo. *See* **Cornalia, Emilio.**

Philippi, R. A.

Zoologische Bemerkungen (Fortsetzung). *Arch. f. Naturgesch.*, VI. 1, pp. 181–195, Taf. III., IV. *1840.*

Trans. in *Ann. Mag. Nat. Hist.*, VI. pp. 89–101, Pl. III., IV. *1841.*

(Zoëa of *Pagurus*, pp. 184–186, Taf. III. figs. 7, 8.)

Kurze Beschreibung einiger neuen Crustaceen. *Arch. f. Naturgesch.*, *1857*, 1, pp. 319–329, Taf. XIV.

(*Thysanopus, Hoplites* [schizopod stage of *Caridea*], *Lucifer, Alima, Euacanthus* [zoën of *Porcellana*], *Megalopa* [*Cancer?* see Gerstaecker, *Arch. f. Naturgesch.*, *1858*, 2, p. 455].)

Plateau, Félix.

Recherches sur les Crustacés d'Eau douce de Belgique.

1° Partie. Genres *Gammarus, Linceus* et *Cypris. Mém. Cour. Acad. Roy. Belgique*, XXXIV. *1868.* 66 pp., 1 pl.

2° et 3° Parties. Genres *Daphnia, Bosmina, Polyphemus, Cyclopsina, Canthocamptus* et *Cyclops. Ibid.* XXXV. *1870.* 92 pp., 3 pl.

(Development, pp. 75–82.)

Power, Wilmot Henry. *See* **Bate, C. Spence.**

Prevost, Bénédict.

*Histoire d'un Insecte (ou d'un Crustacé) qui l'Auteur a cru devoir appeler Chirocéphale diaphane (*Branchiopode* Lam., *Cancer stagnalis* L., *Gammarus stagn.* Fabr.). *Journ. de Physique*, LVII. pp. 37–54, 89–106, Pl. I. *1803.*

Appears, in substance, in JURINE's *Histoire des Monocles*, pp. 201–244, *1820.*

Mémoire sur le Chirocéphale. In JURINE's *Histoire des Monocles*, pp. 201–244, Pl. XX.–XXII. *1820.*

(Young, pp. 214–220, Pl. XX., XXI.)

Rasch.

*Om Forsog med kunstig Udklackning af Hummer. *Nordisk Tidsskrift for Fiskeri*, ny Række, 2en Aargang, pp. 184, 188. *1875*.

Translated in *United States Commission of Fish and Fisheries*. Part III. *Report of the Commissioner for 1873-74 and 1874-75*, pp. 267-269. Washington, *1876*.

 (Observations of Professor Rasch on young *Homarus*, pp. 268, 269.)

Rathke, Heinrich.

Flusskrebs. *Isis, 1825*, 2, col. 1093-1099.

 (Prodromus of complete memoir published in *1829*).

 See also account of the development of *Astacus*, by RATHKE, in BUR-DACH's *Physiologie*, II. pp. 191-200, Leipzig, *1828*, and *Isis, 1829*, col. 429, 430.

Untersuchungen über die Bildung und Entwickelung des Flusskrebses. Leipzig, *1829*. 97 pp., 5 pl.

 Abstract in *Ann. Sci. Nat.*, XX. pp. 442-469, Pl. V.-VIII. *1830*. *Zoölog. Journ.*, V. pp. 241-255. *1830*. Milne Edwards's *Hist. Nat. des Crustacés*, I. pp. 175-195, Pl. XIV. Paris, *1834*.

Abhandlungen zur Bildungs- und Entwickelungs-Geschichte des Menschen und der Thiere. Leipzig, *1832-33*. 216 pp., 14 pl.

 1er Th. 1o Abh. Untersuchungen über die Bildung und Entwickelung der Wasser-Assel oder des *Oniscus aquaticus*. Pp. 1-20, Pl. 1. *1832*.

 Also in *Ann. Sci. Nat.* [2], Zool., II. pp. 139-157, Pl. II. C. *1834*.

 2er Th. 2e Abh. Bildungs- und Entwickelungs-Geschichte des *Oniscus asellus* oder der Kellar-Assel. Pp. 69-84, Pl. VI. *1833*.

 2er Th. 3te Abh. Bildungs- und Entwickelungs-Geschichte einiger Entomostraken (*Daphnia Pulex, Lynceus sphaericus, Cyclops quadricornis*). Pp. 85-94, Pl. VII. figs. 1-5. *1833*.

Ueber die Entwickelung der Decapoden. *Arch. f. Anat. Physiol. und wissensch. Medicin (Müller's)*, *1836*, pp. 187-192.

 Trans. in *Edinburgh New Philosoph. Journ.*, XXII. pp. 364-366. *1837*.

 (This is a preliminary notice of the observations published in *Zur Morphologie*, &c.)

Zur Morphologie, Reisebemerkungen aus Taurien. Riga u. Leipzig, *1837*. 192 pp., 5 pl.

 Dritte Abhandlung. Zur Entwickelungsgeschichte der Crustaceen. Pp. 35-151, 179-184, Tab. I. figs. 13-15, II.-IV.

 (*Lernæopoda, Bopyrus, Idothea, Ligia, Janira, Amphithoë, Gammarus, Crangon, Palæmon, Eriphia, Carcinus.*)

Beobachtungen und Betrachtungen über die Entwickelung der *Mysis vulgaris*. *Arch. f. Naturgesch.*, *1839*, 1, pp. 195-210, Taf. VI.

Zur Entwickelungsgeschichte der Dekapoden. *Arch. f. Naturgesch.*, VI. 1, pp. 241-249. *1840.*

Trans. by W. Francis in *Ann. Mag. Nat. Hist.*, VI. pp. 263-269. *1841.*

(*Astacus [Homarus] marinus, Pagurus Bernhardus, Galatea rugosa, Ilyas araneus.*)

(This is an abstract of the observations published in *Reisebemerkungen aus Skandinarien*, &c.)

Beiträge zur vergleichenden Anatomie und Physiologie, Reisebemerkungen aus Skandinavien, nebst einem Anhange über die rückschreitende Metamorphose der Thiere. *Neueste Schriften der naturforschenden Gesellschaft in Danzig*, III. Heft 4, *1842.* 162 pp., 6 pl.

II. Zur Entwickelungs-Geschichte der Dekapoden. Pp. 23-55, Tab. II. figs. 11-21, III., IV.

(*Homarus, Pagurus, Galatea, Ilyas.*)

Beiträge zur Fauna Norwegens. *Nov. Act. Acad. Cæs. Leop.-Car. Nat. Cur.*, XX. pp. 1-264 c, Tab. I.-XII. *1843.*

(Development of *Phryxus*, pp. 49-56, Taf. I. figs. 16, 17; *Nicothoë*, pp. 109-116, Taf. V. figs. 7-10.)

Reichenbach, Heinrich.

Die Embryonalanlage und erste Entwicklung des Flusskrebses. *Zeitschr. f. wissensch. Zool.*, XXIX. 123-196, 263-266, Taf. X.-XII. *1877.*

(*Vorläufige Mittheilung* appeared in **Centralblatt für die medizin. Wissenschaften*, 1876, No. 41.)

Abstr. by P. Mayer in *Jahresber. üb. Fortschr. Anat. u. Physiol.*, VI. (1877), 2e Abth. pp. 162-164. *1878.*

Eng. Abstr. by T. Jeffery Parker in *Quart. Journ. Microscop. Sci.* [2], XVIII. pp. 84-91. *1878.*

Richiardi, S.

Sulle Sacculine. *Atti della Soc. Toscana di Scienze Nat.*, I. fasc. 2°. *1875.*

(Contains observations on development.)

Descrizione di cinque Specie Nuove del Genere *Philichthys* ed una di *Sphærifer*. *Atti della Soc. Toscana di Scienze Nat.*, III. Tav. VI. *1877.*

(Nauplius of *Sphærifer Leydigi*, fig. 8.)

Descrizione di due Specie Nuove di *Lernæenicus* Les., con Osservazioni intorno a questo ed ai Generi *Lernæocera* Bl., e *Lernæonema* M. Edw. *Atti della Soc. Toscana di Scienze Nat.*, III. Tav. VII. *1877.*

(Describes and figures young forms of *Lernæenicus.*)

Richters, Ferd.

Die Phyllosomen. Ein Beitrag zur Entwicklungsgeschichte der Loricaten. *Zeitschr. f. wissensch. Zool.*, XXIII. pp. 623-646, Taf. XXXI.-XXXIV. *1873.*

Rösel von Rosenhof, August Johann.

Der monatlich-herausgegebenen Insecten-Belustigung Dritter Theil. Nürnberg, *1755*. 624 pp., 101 pl.

(Young of *Astacus*, p. 337; *Gammarus*, p. 353.)

Rougemont, Ph. de.

Étude de la Faune des Eaux privées de Lumière. Histoire Naturelle du *Gammarus puteanus* Koch. Description de l'*Asellus Sieboldii*. Observations anatomiques sur l'*Hydrobia* de Munich. Paris, *1876*. 49 pp., 5 pl.

(Describes six forms of *Gammarus puteanus*, pp. 28–31, Pl. I.–III.)

Sur l'Anatomie des Organes génitaux de l'Écrevisse de Rivière (*Astacus fluviatilis* Rond.) et sur la Physiologie de la Génération de ces Crustacés. *Bull. Soc. Sci. Nat. Neuchatel*, XI. pp. 400–402. *1879*.

(Observations on young.)

Saint George. *See* **La Valette St. George.**

Saint-Hilaire. *See* **Geoffroy Saint-Hilaire.**

Salensky, W.

Sphaeronalla Leuckarti, ein neuer Schmarotzerkrebs. *Arch. f. Naturgesch. 1868*, 1, pp. 301–322, Taf. X.

(Gives account of development. Parasitic Copepod.)

Sars, Georg Ossian.

Norges Ferskvandskrebsdyr. Første Afsnit *Branchiopoda*. I. *Cladocera Ctenopoda* (Fam. *Sididæ & Holopedidæ*). (Prisbelønnet Afhandling.) Christiania, *1865*. viii. + 71 pp., 4 pl.

(Young of *Sida crystallina*, Tab. I. figs. 3–7.)

Histoire Naturelle des Crustacés d'Eau douce de Norvège. 1e Livraison. Les Malacostracés. Christiania, *1867*. 146 pp., 10 pl.

(Development of *Gammarus neglectus*, pp. 64, 66, Pl. VI. figs. 10–19; *Asellus aquaticus*, pp. 116–122, Pl. X. figs. 23–40.)

Carcinologiske Bidrag til Norges Fauna. I. Monographi over de ved Norges Kyster forekommende Mysider. Første Hefte. Christiania, *1870*. 64 pp., 5 pl.

(Embryo of *Pseudomma roseum*, Tab. IV. fig. 23.)

Om en dimorph Udvikling samt Generationsvexel hos *Leptodora*. *Forhandl. Vidensk.-Selsk. Christiania*, Aar 1873, pp. 1–15, Tab. I. *1873*.

Notice of, by S. I. SMITH, in *Amer. Journ. Sci. & Arts* [3], IX. pp. 230, 231. Mar. *1875*.

Om Hummerens postembryonale Udvikling. *Forhandl. Vidensk.-Selsk. Christiania*, Aar 1874, pp. 1–27, Tab. I., II. *1875*.

Abstr. in *Gervais's Journ. de Zool.*, IV. pp. 362, 363. *1875*.

Notice of, by S. I. SMITH, in *Amer. Journ. Sci. & Arts* [3], IX. p. 231. Mar. *1875*.

(Three larval stages of *Homarus vulgaris*.)

Sars, Michael.

Beskrivelse over *Lophogaster typicus*, en mærkværdig Form af de lavere tifⱷddede Krebsdyr. *Kongl. Norske Universitetsprogram for andet Halvaar* 1862. Christiania, *1862.* iv. + 37 pp., 3 pl.

Abstr. in *Bibliothèque Univ., Arch. Sci. Phys. Nat.,* XXI. pp. 87, 88. *1864. Ann. Mag. Nat. Hist.* [3], XIV. pp. 461, 462. *1864.*

(Development, pp. iv, 21-25, Tab. III. figs. 57-65.)

Bidrag til Kundskab om Christianiafjordens Fauna. Christiania, [I.] *1868 ;* II. *1870.* 218 pp., 13 pl.

(Young of *Munnopsis typica* [I.], Pl. VII. figs. 137, 138 ; nauplius of *Melinnacheres ergasiloides*, II. p. 14, Pl. VIII. fig. 7 ; embryo and nauplius of *Anteacheres Duebenii*, pp. 26-28, Pl. X. figs. 35-37.)

Say, Thomas.

An Account of the Crustacea of the United States. *Journ. Acad. Nat. Sci. Phila.,* I. pp. 155-169. *1817.*

(The megalopa of *Ocypoda* described as a Macrouran genus under the name of *Monolepis,* pp. 155-160.)

Schäffer, Jacob Christian.

Die grünen Armpolypen, die geschwänzten und ungeschwänzten zackigen Wasserflöhe, und eine besondere Art kleiner Wasseraale. Regensburg, *1755.* 94 pp. 3 pl.

Trans. in JURINE's *Histoire des Monocles,* pp. 196, 197. Genève, *1820.*

(Development of *Daphnia,* pp. 56 *et seq.,* Pl. I. figs. 2, 3.)

*Der Krebsartige Kiefenfuss mit der kurzen und langen Schwanzklappe. Regensburg, *1756.*

(Parthenogenesis in *Apus cancriformis* and *A. productus.*)

Schiödte (Jörgen C.) [and Meinert (Fr.)].

Sur la Propagation et les Métamorphoses des Crustacés suceurs de la Famille des Cymothoadiens. *Comptes Rendus de l'Acad. des Sci., Paris,* LXXXVII. pp. 52-55. *1878.*

Trans. in *Ann. Mag. Nat. Hist.* [5], II. pp. 195-197. *1878.*

Schmankewitsch, Wladimir.

*[On some Crustacea from Salt Lakes and Fresh Waters, and their Relation to the surrounding Element.] *Zapiski Novoross. Obshtch. Yestestvoisp.* [*Mem. New-Russian Soc. of Naturalists*], III. 2. *1875.* (In Russian.)

Ueber das Verhältniss der *Artemia salina* Miln. Edw. zur *Artemia Mühlhausenii* Miln. Edw. und dem Genus *Branchipus* Schaeff. *Zeitschr. f. wissensch. Zool.,* Supplem. XXV. pp. 103-116, Taf. VI. *1875.*

Trans. in *Ann. Mag. Nat. Hist.* [4], XVII. pp. 256-258. *1876.*

Zur Kenntniss des Einflusses der äusseren Lebensbedingungen auf die Organisation der Thiere. *Zeitschr. f. wissensch. Zool.,* XXIX. pp. 429-494. *1877.*

(On the influence of salt and fresh waters on the development of Crustacea.)

Schmidt, Oscar.

Zoologische Mittheilungen. *Zeitschr. gesammt. Naturwissen.*, II. p. 101, *1853.*
Hand-Atlas d. vergl. Anat., Taf. X. fig. 7. *1853.* *Das Weltall*, No. 3,
p. 19. *1854.*

(*Peltogaster* shown to be a parasitic Crustacean from its development.)

Schöbl, Jos.

Ueber die Fortpflanzung isopoder Crustaceen. *Arch. f. Mikroskop. Anat.*, XVII.
pp. 125–140, Taf. IX., X. *1879.* *Sitzungsber. böhm. Gesell. Wissensch.
1879,* pp. 339–350.

Schulze, Max.

Zoologische Skizzen. *Zeitschr. f wissensch. Zool.*, IV. pp. 178–195. *1852.*

(Development of *Balanidæ*, pp. 190–192.)

Semper, Carl.

Reisebericht von Herrn Dr. Carl Semper. Briefliche Mittheilung an A. Kölliker. *Zeitschr. f. wissensch. Zool.*, XIII. pp. 558–570, Taf. XXXVIII.,
XXXIX. *1863.*

(Larva of *Sacculina*, p. 560, Taf. XXXVIII. figs. 3ᵃ, 3ᵇ.)

On the Embryogeny of the *Rhizocephala. Ann. Mag. Nat. Hist.* [4], XV.
pp. 83, 84. *1875. Arch. Zool. Expér.*, IV. pp. viii., ix. *1875.*

(Reply to GIARD.)

*Die natürlichen Existenzbedinguugen der Thiere. Leipzig, *1880* [Ausge-
geben, *1879*]. 2 vols., 299 + 296 pp. (Internat. wissensch. Biblio-
thek.)

English trans.: Animal Life as affected by the Natural Conditions of
Existence. London and New York, *1881.* 472 pp., 106 cuts. (Interna-
tional Scientific Series.)

(Zoëa of *Pinnotheres holothuriæ*, p. 81, fig. 22. Influence of temperature and
desiccation on development of eggs of *Apus, Branchipus, Cypris*, pp. 129, 175, 176.)

Shaw, George.

Description of the *Cancer stagnalis* of Linnæus. *Trans. Linn. Soc. London*, I.
pp. 103–110, Pl. IX. *1791.*

(*Branchipus.* Describes eggs and young.)

Siebold, C. Th. E. v.

Beiträge zur Parthenogenesis der Arthropoden. Leipzig, *1871.* 238 pp., 2 pl.
VI. Ueber die parthenogenetische Fortpflanzung bei *Apus* und verwandten
Crustaceen. Pp. 160–222, Taf. II.

(*Apus cancriformis, Apus productus, Artemia salina, Limnadia Hermanni.*)

Ueber Parthenogenesis der *Artemia salina. Sitzungsber. d. Königl. Akad. d.
Wissensch. zu München,* III. pp. 168–196. *1873.*

Slabber, Mart.

*Natuurkundige Verlustigingen, behelzende microscopische Waarnemingen van
in- en uit- landische Water- en Land-Dieren. Haarlem, *1769–78.*

*German trans. by P. L. St. Müller : Physikalische Belustigungen, oder microscopische Wahrnehmungen in- und ausländischer Wasser- und Land-Thieren. Nürnberg, *1775-81*.

(Cirriped larva, zoöa of *Brachyura*, &c. See Bell's *Hist. Brit. Stalk-eyed Crustacea*, Introd., pp. xxxix. *et seqq.*: J. V. Thompson's *Zoölog. Res.*, Mem. I., and copy of figs. in *Encyc. Méth.*, Pl. CCLXVII., CCCXXXIII.; Latreille's *Hist. Nat. gen. et partic. des Crustacés et des Insectes*, IV., Pl. XXXXV., &c.)

Smith, Sidney I.

The Early Stages of the American Lobster (*Homarus Americanus* Edwards). *Amer. Journ. Sci. & Arts*, [3], III. pp. 401-406, Pl. IX. *1872*.

(Abstract of later paper in *Trans. Conn. Acad.*)

The Early Stages of the American Lobster (*Homarus Americanus* Edwards). *Trans. Conn. Acad.*, II. pp. 351-381, Pl. XIV.-XVIII. *1873*.

(Includes description of larva of *Palæmonetes vulgaris*, p. 377, foot-note.)

The Metamorphoses of the Lobster and other Crustacea. *Invert. Animals of Vineyard Sound, etc.* (Verrill and Smith), pp. 228-243, Pl. VIII., IX. *Rep. U. S. Fish Comm.* 1871-72, pp. 522-537. Washington, *1873*.

(*Homarus, Crangon, Palæmonetes, Virbius, Gebia, Callianassa, Eupagurus, Hippa, Cancer, Platyonychus, Cyllene, Ocypoda, Gelasimus?, Squilla*, &c., noticed.)

The Megalops Stage of *Ocypoda*. *Amer. Journ. Sci. & Arts* [3], VI. pp. 67, 68. *1873*.

(*Monolepis inermis* Say is the megalopa of *Ocypoda arenaria*.)

The Early Stages of *Hippa talpoida*, with a Note on the Structure of the Mandibles and Maxillæ in *Hippa* and *Remipes*. *Trans. Conn. Acad.*, III. pp. 311-342, Pl. XLV.-XLVIII. *1877*.

The Stalk-eyed Crustaceans of the Atlantic Coast of North America north of Cape Cod. *Trans. Conn. Acad.*, V. pp. 27-136, Pl. VIII.-XII. *1879*.

(Observations on larval stages of *Thysanopoda*, pp. 90, 91.)

On the Species of *Pinnixa* inhabiting the New England Coast, with Remarks on their Early Stages. *Trans. Conn. Acad.*, IV. pp. 247-253. July, *1880*.

Occasional Occurrence of Tropical and Sub-tropical Species of Decapod Crustacea on the Coast of New England. *Trans. Conn. Acad.*, IV. pp. 254-267. July, *1880*.

(Describes megalopa stage of *Calappa marmorata*, &c.)

Soubeiran, Léon.

Sur l'Histoire Naturelle et l'Education des Écrevisses. *Comptes Rendus de l'Acad. des Sci.*, Paris, LX. pp. 1249, 1250. *1865*.

Spangenberg, Friedrich.

Zur Kenntniss von *Branchipus stagnalis*. *Zeitschr. f. wissensch. Zool.*, Supplem. XXV. pp. 1-64, Taf. I.-III. *1875*.

(Contains observations on development.)

Steenstrup [Joh. Japetus Smith].

Bemærkninger om Slægterne *Pachybdella* Dies. og *Peltogaster* Rathk. *Overs. K. Danske Vidensk. Selsk. Forhandl. 1854*, pp. 145–158, 214.

Trans. by CREPLIN in *Arch. f. Naturgesch. 1855*, 1, pp. 15–29, 62.

English trans. in *Ann. Mag. Nat. Hist.* [2], XVI. pp. 153–162. *1855*.

[On *Liriope* and *Peltogaster*.] *Forhandl. Skand. Naturforsk.*, VIII. (1860), pp. 684, 685. Kiöbenhavn, *1861*.

Steffenberg, Adalrik.

*Bidrag til Kännedomen om Flodkräftans Naturalhistoria. Falun, *1872*. 72 pp. (Akadem. Afhandl.)

Noticed by EDUARD VON MARTENS in *Zoölog. Rec.* (1872), IX. p. 193. *1874*.

(Young of *Astacus fluviatilis*.)

St. George. *See* **La Valette St. George.**

Straus-Durckheim, Hercule Eug.

Mémoire sur les *Daphnia*, de la Classe des Crustacés. *Mém. du Mus. d'Hist. Nat.*, V. pp. 380–425, Pl. XXIX., *1819 ;* VI. pp. 149–162, *1820*.

(Contains observations on development.)

Mémoire sur les *Cypris*, de la Classe des Crustacés. *Mém. du Mus. d'Hist. Nat.*, VII. pp. 33–61, Pl. I. *1821*.

(Young, p. 54.)

Stuxberg, Anton.

Karcinologiska Iakttagelser. *Öfvers. K. Svenska Vetensk.-Akad. Förhandl.*, XXX. (1873), No. 9, pp. 3–23, Taf. XIV. *1874*.

(*Stenorrhynchus rostratus, Carcinus Mænas, Portunus depurator, Galatea inter-media, Hippolyte varians, Pakemon squilla, Pachybdella carcini*.)

Suhm. *See* **Willemoes-Suhm.**

Targioni Tozzetti, Ad.

Di una Specie nuova in un nuovo Genere di Cirripedi Lepadidei ospitante sulle Penne abdominali del *Priofinus cinereus* dell' Atlantico Australe e dell' Oceano Indiano raccolta nel Viaggio intorno al Mondo della Fregata Italiana *La Magenta* dai Professori F. De Filippi ed E. Giglioli. *Bull. Soc. Ento-molog. Italiana*, IV. pp. 84–96, Tav. I. figs. 2–13. *1872*.

(*Ornitholepas australis*, young stage according to A. GERSTAECKER, *Sitzungs-Ber. Gesell. naturforsch. Freunde Berlin, 1875*, pp. 113–115.)

Thompson, John V.

Zoölogical Researches and Illustrations; or Natural History of nondescript or imperfectly known Animals, in a Series of Memoirs. Illustrated by Numerous Figures. Cork, *1828–34*. 110 pp., 20 pl.

Memoir I. On the Metamorphoses of the Crustacea, and on Zoëa, ex-posing their singular Structure and demonstrating that they are not, as has been supposed, a peculiar Genus, but the Larva of Crustacea. Pp. 1–11, Pl. I., II. Addenda, pp. 63–65, Pl. VIII. fig. 1.

Analyt. notice in *Zoölog. Journ.*, IV. pp. 248–250. *1828.*

(*Cancer pagurus*, &c.)

Memoir II. On the Genus *Mysis* or Opossum Shrimp. Pp. 13–31, Pl. III., IV. Addendum, p. 66.

(Contains observations on development.)

Memoir IV. On the Cirripedes or Barnacles; demonstrating their deceptive Character; the extraordinary Metamorphosis they undergo, and the Class of Animals to which they indisputably belong. Pp. 69–82, Pl. IX., X.

(*Balanus.*)

Memoir VI. Development of *Artemis salinus* or Brine Shrimp; demonstrative of its Relationship to *Branchipus* and the other Crustaceous *Phyllopoda*, and to those enigmatical Fossils, the apparently eyeless Trilobites .... with a new Species of *Artemis* and of *Apus*. Pp. 103–110, Pl. I.–VI.

[Letter to the Editor of the Zoölogical Journal, dated "Cork, Dec. 16, 1830."] *Zoölog. Journ.*, V. pp. 383, 384, Pl. XV. fig. 13. *1831.*

(Metamorphosis of *Homarus*.)

Discovery of the Metamorphosis in the Second Type of the Cirripedes, viz., the *Lepades*, completing the Natural History of these singular Animals, and confirming their Affinity with the Crustacea. *Phil. Trans. Roy. Soc. London, 1835*, pp. 355–358, Pl. VI.

On the Double Metamorphosis in the Decapodous Crustacea, exemplified in *Cancer Mænas* Linn. *Phil. Trans. Roy. Soc. London, 1835*, pp. 359–362, Pl. V.

Memoir on the Metamorphosis and Natural History of the *Pinnotheres* or Pea-Crabs. *Entomolog. Mag.*, III. pp. 85–90, figs. 1–3. April, *1835.*

Memoir on the Metamorphosis in *Porcellana* and *Portunus*. *Entomolog. Mag.*, III. pp. 275–280, figs. 1–3. October, *1835.*

Of the Double Metamorphosis in *Macropodia phalangium* or Spider-Crab, with Proofs of the Larvæ being Zoëa in *Gecarcinus hydrodomus*, *Telphusa erythropus*, *Eriphia Caribbæa*, and *Grapsus pelagicus*. *Entomolog. Mag.*, III. pp. 370–375, figs. 1–6. January, *1836.*

Natural History and Metamorphosis of an anomalous Crustaceous Parasite of *Carcinus Mænas*, the *Sacculina carcini*. *Entomolog. Mag.*, III. pp. 452–456, figs. 1–6. April, *1836.*

Notice of, in *Arch. f. Naturgesch.*, *1837*, 2, p. 248.

Memoir on the Metamorphosis in the *Macroura* or Long-tailed Crustacea, exemplified in the Prawn (*Palæmon serratus*). *Edinburgh New Philosoph. Journ.*, XXI. pp. 221–223, Pl. I. *1836.*

Abstract in *Proc. Roy. Soc.*, III. p. 371. *1836.*

238 BULLETIN OF THE

Thompson, William.

Description of a Young Lobster measuring only Nine Lines. *The Zoölogist,* XI. p. 3765. *1853.*

Thorell, T.

Bidrag till Kännedomen om Krustaceer, som lefva i Arter af Slägtet *Ascidia* L. 84 pp., 14 pl. *K. Svenska Vetensk.-Akad. Handl.,* III. No. 8. *1859–60.* *Zeitschr. gesammt. Naturwissen.,* XV. pp. 114–143. *1860.*
(*Copepoda.* Young, *passim.*)

Till Kännedomen om Vissa parasitiskt lefvande Entomostraceer. *Öfvers. K. Svenska Vetensk.-Akad. Förhandl.,* XVI. (1859), pp. 335–362. *1860.*
(Includes account of development.)

Tozzetti. *See* **Targioni Tozzetti.**

Travis.

[Letter to Pennant, dated "Scarborough, 25th Oct. 1768."] PENNANT's *British Zoölogy,* IV. pp. 11–15. London, *1777.*
(Describes the eggs of *Homarus.* Young have "the appearance of tadpoles.")

Tscherniawsky, W.

*Materialia ad Zoographiam Ponticam comparatam, Basis Genealogiæ Crustaceorum. Oct. *1868.* 120 pp., 8 pl. (In Russian.)
Noticed by GERSTAECKER in *Arch. f. Naturgesch.,* 1869. 2, p. 168.
(Larva of *Balanus,* and three zoëæ.)

*[The Megalopa Larvæ of *Brachyura.*] *Trudy Russkoye Entomolog. Obshtchest.* [*Trans. Russian Entomolog. Soc.*], XI. No. 2, pp. 51–96, 2 pl. *1878.* (In Russian.)
See *Zoolog. Anzeig.,* II. p. 219. *1879. Zoölog. Rec.* (1878), XV., Crust., pp. 15, 16. *1880.*
Notice of, by PAUL MAYER, in *Zoolog. Jahresber.* 1880, II. Abth., pp. 41, 42. *1881.*

Ueber die Genealogie der Mysiden. *Zoolog. Anzeig.,* III. pp. 213, 214. *1880.*
(*Verhandl. d. zool. Sect. d. VI. Versamml. russisch. Naturf. u. Aerzte.*)
Eng. abstr. in *Journ. Roy. Microscop. Soc.,* III. pp. 944, 945. *1880.*

Turner (Wm.) and Wilson (H. S.).

On the Structure of the *Chondracanthus lophii,* with Observations on its Larval Form. *Trans. Roy. Soc. Edinburgh,* XXIII. pp. 67–76, Pl. III. *1861.*
Abstr. in *Proc. Roy. Soc. Edinburgh,* IV. pp. 525–527. *1862.*
(Larva, pp. 74, 75, Pl. III. figs. 15, 16.)

On the Structure of *Lernæopoda Dalmanni,* with Observations on its Larval Form. *Trans. Roy. Soc. Edinburgh,* XXIII. pp. 77–87, Pl. IV. *1861.*
Abstr. in *Proc. Roy. Soc. Edinburgh,* IV. pp. 569, 570. *1862.*
(Larva, pp. 84, 85, figs. 13–16.)

Uljanin, B.

Untersuchungen über Blastoderm- und Keimblätterbildung bei *Orchestia Montagui* und *mediterranea*. *Zoolog. Anzeig.*, III. pp. 163–165. *1880.* (*Verhandl. d. zoolog. Sect. d. VI. Versamml. russisch. Naturf. u. Aerzte.*)

Notice of, by P. MAYER, in *Zoolog. Jahresber.* (1880), II. Abt., pp. 53, 54. *1880.*

Zur Entwicklungsgeschichte der Amphipoden. *Zeitschr. f. wissensch. Zool.*, XXXV. pp. 440–460, Taf. XXIV. *1881.*

Abstr. in *Journ. Roy. Microscop. Soc.* [2], I. pp. 599, 600. Aug. *1881.*

Valenciennes, A.

Note sur la Reproduction des Homards. *Comptes Rendus de l'Acad. des Sci.*, *Paris*, XLVI. pp. 603–606. *1858.*

Valette St. George. *See* **La Valette St. George.**

Van Beneden, Édouard.

Sur le Mode de Formation de l'Œuf et le Développement embryonnaire des Sacculines. *Comptes Rendus de l'Acad. des Sci.*, *Paris*, LXIX. pp. 1146–1151. 29 Nov. *1869.*

Trans. in *Ann. Mag. Nat. Hist.* [4], V. pp. 140–144. *1870.*

Recherches sur l'Embryogénie des Crustacés. I. Observations sur le Développement de l'*Asellus aquaticus*. *Bull. Acad. Roy. de Belgique* [2], XXVIII. pp. 54–87, 2 pl. *1869.*

Recherches sur l'Embryogénie des Crustacés. II. Développement des *Mysis*. *Bull. Acad. Roy. de Belgique* [2], XXVIII. pp. 232–249, 1 pl. *1869.*

Recherches sur l'Embryogénie des Crustacés. III. Développement de l'Œuf et de l'Embryon des Sacculines (*Sacculina carcini*, Thomps.). *Bull. Acad. Roy. de Belgique* [2], XXIX. pp. 99–112, 1 pl. *1870.*

Recherches sur l'Embryogénie des Crustacés. IV. Développement des Genres *Anchorella*, *Lernæopoda*, *Brachiella* et *Hessia*. *Bull. Acad. Roy. de Belgique* [2], XXIX. pp. 223–254, 1 pl. *1870.*

Réponse à quelques-unes des Observations de M. Balbiani sur l'Œuf des Sacculines. *Comptes Rendus de l'Acad. des Sci.*, *Paris*, LXX. pp. 197–200. *1870.*

Recherches sur la Composition et la Signification de l'Œuf, basées sur l'Étude de son Mode de Formation et des premières Phénomènes embryonnaires (Mammifères, Oiseaux, Crustacés, Vers). *Mém. Cour. Acad. Roy. de Belgique*, XXXIV. *1870* [*1869?*]. 283 pp., 12 pl.

(Crustacea, pp. 107–143, Pl. VII.–X.)

Van Beneden (Édouard) et Bessels (Émile).

Mémoire sur la Formation du Blastoderme chez les Amphipodes, les Lernéens et les Copépodes. *Mém. Cour. Acad. Roy. de Belgique*, XXXIV. *1870* [*1868?*]. 59 pp., 5 pl.

Résumé in *Bull. Acad. Roy. de Belgique* [2], XXV. pp. 434–448. *1868. Monthly Microscop. Journ.*, 1. pp. 41–43. Jan. *1869.*

See also Report by SCHWANN, GLUGE, and POELMAN, *Bull. Acad. Roy. de Belgique* [2], XXVI. pp. 252–259. *1868.*

Van Beneden, P.-J.

Résumé d'un Mémoire sur le Développement et l'Organisation des Nicothoés. *Bull. Acad. Roy. de Belgique*, XV. 2ᵐᵉ Partie, pp. 386–390. *1848. Schleiden u. Froriep's Notizen* [3], IX. col. 165–167. *1849.*

Mémoire sur le Développement et l'Organisation des Nicothoés. *Mém. Acad. Roy. de Belgique*, XXIV. *1850.* 28 pp., 1 pl. *Ann. Sci. Nat.* [3], Zool., XIII. pp. 354–377, Pl. I. figs. 13–29. *1850.*

Recherches sur quelques Crustacés inférieurs. *Ann. Sci. Nat.* [3], Zool., XVI. pp. 71–131, Pl. II.-VI. *1851.*

(Parasitic *Copepoda*, Lernæans.)

Note sur un nouveau Genre de Crustacé parasite, *Eudactylina. Bull. Acad. Roy. de Belgique*, XX. Pt. I. pp. 235–238, 1 pl. *1853.*

(Larvæ, figs. 5, 6.)

Histoire naturelle d'un Animal nouveau, désigné sous le Nom d'*Histriobdella. Bull. Acad. Roy. de Belgique, 1858*, pp. 263–296.

(Development of *Homarus*, pp. 263, 264.)

Un nouveau Genre de Crustacé Lernéen. *Bull. Acad. Roy. de Belgique, 1860*, pp. 137–146, 1 pl.

(*Enterocola fulgens* P. J. Van Ben. Larva, figs. 6, 7.)

Recherches sur les Crustacés du Littoral de Belgique. *Mém. Acad. Roy. de Belgique*, XXXIII. *1861* [*1860?*]. 174 pp., 21 pl.

Also printed separately with the following title: Recherches sur la Faune littorale de Belgique. Crustacés. Bruxelles, *1861.* 174 pp., 21 pl.

See Rev. by FRITZ MÜLLER, *Ueber Cumaceen. Arch. f. Naturgesch., 1865*, 1, pp. 311–323.

(Development of *Mysis*, pp. 52–69, Pl. VI. figs. 9–12, VIII.-XI.; *Homarus*, p. 53; *Cuma*, pp. 75, 87; *Cyamus*, p. 95; *Anceus*, p. 102, Pl. XVI.; *Peltogaster*, p. 118, Pl. XXI. figs. 5–7; *Sacculina*, Pl. XX. figs. 8, 9, Pl. XXI. figs. 8,•9; *Lernæa*, p. 131, Pl. XIX. figs. 9–13.)

Vejdovský, Franz.

Untersuchungen über die Anatomie und Metamorphose von *Tracheliastes polycolpus* Nordm. *Zeitschr. f. wissensch. Zool.*, XXIX. pp. 15–46, Taf. II.-IV. *1877.*

(Development, pp. 34–43, Taf. III.', IV.)

Vogt, Carl.

Recherches Cotières. Genève, *1877.* 104 pp., 6 pl. *Mém. Inst. Genève*, XIII.

1ᵉʳ Mém. De la Famille des Philichthydes et en particulier du Lépo-
sphile des Labres (*Lrposphilus labrei* Hesse). Pp. 1–41, Pl. I., II.

(Nauplius, p. 26, Pl. I. fig. 10.)

2ᵈ Mém. Sur quelques Copépodes Parasites à Males Pygmées habitant
les Poissons. Pp. 43–104, Pl. III.–VI.

(Nauplius of *Brachiella*, p. 56, Pl. III. fig. 8; *Chondracanthus*, pp. 86–88, Pl. V.)

Also in *Arch. Zool. Expér.*, VI. 385–456. *1877.*

Recherches Cotières faites a Roskoff. Crustacés Parasites des Poissons.
Genève, *1879.* 104 pp., 6 pl.

1ᵉʳ Mém. Leposphile des Labres, Famille des Philichthydes.

2ᵈ Mém. Familles des Lernæopodides et des Chondracanthides.

(Nauplius of *Leposphilus, Brachiella, Chondracanthus.*)

Same as the preceding.

L'Adaptation des Crustacés Copépodes au Parasitisme. *Actes de la Soc.
Helvétique des Sci. Nat.*, 60ᵉ Sess., pp. 121–139. *1878.*

(Contains remarks on larvæ.)

Wagner, Nicolas.

Observations sur l'Organisation et le Développement des Ancées. *Bull. Acad.
Impér. des Sci., de St.-Pétersbourg*, X. pp. 498–502 (*Mélanges Biologiques*,
VI. pp. 27–34). *1866.*

*In *Arbeit. d. ersten Sitzung Russischer Naturforscher in St. Petersburg, 1868*,
pp. 218–237, Taf. I.–IV.

(Development of *Hyalosoma* [*Leptodora*], according to Gerstaecker, *Arch. f. Naturgesch.*, 1871, 1, p. 351.)

Wagner, Rudolphus.

Prodromus Historiæ Generationis Hominis atque Animalium. Lipsiæ, *1836.*
15 pp., 2 pl.

(Eggs of *Porcellio, Cypris, Balanus, Gammarus, Astacus, Carcinus*, p. 8, Pl. I. figs. 12–17.)

Weismann, August.

Ueber Bau und Lebenserscheinungen von *Leptodora hyalina* Lilljeborg.
Zeitschr. f. wissensch. Zool., XXIV. pp. 349–418, Taf. XXXIII.–
XXXVIII. *1874.*

Zur Naturgeschichte der Daphniden. I. Ueber die Bildung von Wintereiern
bei *Leptodora hyalina*. *Zeitschr. f. wissensch. Zool.*, XXVII. pp. 51–112,
Taf. V.–VII. May, *1876.*

Beiträge zur Naturgeschichte der Daphnoiden. Theil II., III., u. IV.
Zeitschr. f. wissensch. Zool., XXVIII. pp. 93–254, Taf. VII.–XI. Jan.
1877.

II. Die Eibildung bei den Daphnoiden. Pp. 95–175.

III. Die Abhängigkeit der Embryonal-Entwicklung vom Fruchtwasser der Mutter. Pp. 176–211.

IV. Ueber den Einfluss der Begattung auf die Erzeugung von Wintereiern. Pp. 212–240.

Beiträge zur Naturgeschichte der Daphnoiden. VII. Die Entstehung der cyclischen Fortpflanzung bei den Daphnoiden. *Zeitschr. f. wissensch. Zool.*, XXXIII. pp. 111–264. Oct. *1879.*

Parthenogenese bei den Ostracoden. *Zoolog. Anzeig.*, III. pp. 82–84. 23 Feb. *1880. Journ. Roy. Microscop. Soc.*, III. Pt. I. pp. 431, 432. *1880.*

Wendt.

Ueber das Ansetzen der Cirripedien an eisernen Schiffen. *Verhandl. d. Vereins f. naturwissensch. Unterhalt. zu Hamburg*, III. (1876), pp. 31, 32. *1878.*

Westwood, J. O.

Extrait des Recherches sur les Crustacés du Genre Pranize de Leach. *Ann. Sci. Nat.*, XXVII. pp. 316–332, Pl. VI. *1832.*

On the Transformations of the Crustacea. *Rep. Brit. Assoc. Adv. Sci. for 1834,* pp. 608, 609. *1835.*
    (Abstract of the following paper.)

On the supposed Existence of Metamorphoses in the Crustacea. *Phil. Trans. Roy. Soc. London, 1835*, pp. 311–328, Pl. IV.
    Abstract in *Proc. Roy. Soc. London*, III. pp. 341, 342. *1835. London and Edinburgh Philosoph. Mag.* [3]. VII. pp. 210, 211. *1835. Froriep's Notizen*, XLVI. pp. 230, 231. *1835.*
    (*Gecarcinus*, with direct development.)

See also **Bate (C. Spence)** and **Hailstone (S.).**

Willemoes-Suhm, Rudolf von.

On a new Genus of Amphipod Crustaceans. *Proc. Roy. Soc. London*, XXI. pp. 206–208. *1873. Ann. Mag. Nat. Hist.* [4], XI. pp. 389–391. *1873.*
    (*Thaumops pellucida* W.-S. [*Cystisoma Neptuni* Guér.-Mén.] undergoes no metamorphosis after leaving the egg, pp. 207, 208.)

Von der Challenger-Expedition. Briefe an C. Th. E. v. Siebold von R. v. Willemoes-Suhm. I. *Zeitschr. f. wissensch. Zool.*, XXIII. pp. i.–vii. May, *1873.*
    (Embryo of *Thaumops pellucida* W.-S. [*Cystisoma Neptuni* Guér.-Mén., Amphipod] undergoes no metamorphosis, p. vi.)

Von der Challenger-Expedition. Briefe an C. Th. E. v. Siebold von R. v. Willemoes-Suhm. II. *Zeitschr. f. wissensch. Zool.*, XXIV. pp. ix.–xxiii. Oct. *1874.*
    (Young *Isopoda* and *Amphipoda* of Antarctic Islands developed in sacs of parent. Larval stages of the higher Crustacea not found on the surface at Kerguelen's Isl., excepting one small zoëa.)

Von der Challenger-Expedition. Briefe von R. v. Willemoes-Suhm an C. Th. E. v. Siebold. V. *Zeitschr. f. wissensch. Zool.*, XXVI. pp. lix.–lxxv. Dec. *1875.*

(According to a very intelligent fisherman, Menancio Perez, the young *Birgus* on hatching is like the parent in form, p. lxxiii.)

On some Atlantic Crustacea from the "Challenger" Expedition. V. On the Development of a Land Crab. *Trans. Linn. Soc. London* [2], Zool., I. pp. 46–48, Pl. XI. figs. 1–3. *1875.*

(Zoëa of *Cardisoma* from Cape-Verd Isl. Direct development of *Telphusa fluviatilis* from Italy.)

On the Development of *Lepas fascicularis* and the "Archizoëa" of *Cirripedia*. *Phil. Trans. Roy. Soc. London*, CLXVI. pp. 131–154, Pl. X.–XV. *1876.*

'Abstract in *Proc. Roy. Soc. London*, XXIV. pp. 129–132. Dec. *1875*. *Ann. Mag. Nat. Hist.* [4], XVII. pp. 158–161. *1876.*

Preliminary Remarks on the Development of some Pelagic Decapods. *Proc. Roy. Soc. London*, XXIV. pp. 132–134. *1875.* Also in *Ann. Mag. Nat. Hist.* [4], XVII. pp. 162, 163. *1876.*

(*Amphion, Sergestes, Lucifer.*)

Preliminary Report to Professor Wyville Thomson, F. R. S., Director of the Civilian Scientific Staff, on Observations made during the earlier Part of the Voyage of H. M. S. "Challenger." *Proc. Roy. Soc. London*, XXIV. pp. 569–585. *1876.*

(Blind megalopa from 1675 fms., p. 577; *Cardisoma* zoëa, p. 582.)

Von der Challenger-Expedition. Briefe von R. v. Willemoes-Suhm an C. Th. E. v. Siebold. VII. *Zeitschr. f. wissensch. Zool.*, XXVII. pp. xcvii.–cviii. May, *1876.*

(*Sergestes, Lucifer, Lepas*, pp. cvi.–cviii. Same observations as those recorded in *Preliminary Remarks, &c.*, and *On the Development of* Lepas fascicularis, *&c.*)

Wilson, E. B. *See* **Brooks, W. K.**

Wilson, H. S. *See* **Turner, Wm.**

Woodward, Henry.

Art. *Crustacea* in *Encyclopædia Britannica* (9th ed.), VI. pp. 632–666. *1877.*

(General account of development, pp. 643–652. Australian *Dromia*, with direct development, p. 644.)

Zaddach, Ernestus Gustavus.

De Apodis cancriformis Schaeff. Anatome et Historia Evolutionis. Bonnæ, *1841.* 72 pp., 4 pl.

(Development, pp. 55–64, Pl. IV.)

Zenker, Jonathan Carolus.

De Gammari pulicis Fabr. Historiâ Naturali atque Sanguinis Circuitu Commentatio. Jenæ, *1832.* viii. + 28 pp., I pl.

(Remarks on development, p. 17.)

Zenker [Wilhelm].

Monographie der Ostracoden. *Arch.f. Naturgesch. 1854,* 1, pp. 1–87, Taf. I.–VI. figs. 1, 2.

(Development, pp. 57–60.)

Also published as **Anatomisch-systematische Studien über die Krebsthiere (Crustacea).* Berlin, *1854.* 115 pp., 6 pl.

—?

[Notice of *Phyllosoma* hatched from Eggs of *Palinurus vulgaris* at Brighton Aquarium.] *Nature,* VIII. p. 231. *1873. Amer. Journ. Sci. & Arts* [3], VI. p. 229. *1873.*

ADDENDA.

Claus, Carl.

Untersuchungen über die Organisation und Verwandtshaft der Copepoden. (In Auszuge zusammengestellt.) *Würzburg. naturwiss. Zeitschr.,* III. pp. 51–103. *1862.*

(Development, pp. 78–82.)

Dohrn, Anton.

*Studien zur Embryologie der Arthropoden. *1868.* (Habilitationsschrift.)

Hartog, Marcus.

On the Anal Respiration of the *Copepoda. Quart. Journ. Microscop. Sci.* [2], XX. pp. 244, 245. April, *1880. Journ. Roy. Microscop. Soc.,* III. Pt. 2, pp. 632, 632. *1880.*

(Anal respiration in nauplius of *Cyclops* and *Diaptomus,* p. 245.)

On the Respiration of the Crustacea. *Quart. Journ. Microscop. Sci.* [2], XX. p. 485. Oct. *1880. Journ. Roy. Microscop. Soc.,* III. Pt. 2, p. 944. *1880.*

(Anal respiration in zoëæ.)

Kossmann, Robby.

Die Entonisciden. *Mittheil. aus der zoolog. Station zu Neapel,* III. pp. 149–169, Taf. VIII., IX. Dec. 9, *1881*

(Development, pp. 166–168, Taf. VIII., fig. 6.)

Studien über Bopyriden. III. *Jone thoracica* und *Cepon portuni. Mittheil. aus der zoolog. Station zu Neapel,* III. pp. 170–183, Taf. X., XI. Dec. 9, *1881.*

(Young stages described and figured.)

XIPHOSURA (Limulus).

Agassiz, Alexander.

Note on the Habits of young *Limulus*. *Amer. Journ. Sci. & Arts* [3], XV. pp. 75, 76. *1878.* *Ann. Mag. Nat. Hist.* [5], 1. pp. 183, 184. *1878.*

(Swim, feed, and rest on their backs.)

Beneden. *See* **Van Beneden.**

Dohrn, Anton.

Untersuchungen über Bau und Entwickelung der Arthropoden. 12. Zur Embryologie und Morphologie des *Limulus Polyphemus*. *Jenaische Zeitschr.,* VI. pp. 580–640, Taf. XIV., XV. *1871.*

Edwards. *See* **Milne Edwards.**

Gegenbaur, C.

Anatomische Untersuchung eine *Limulus*, mit besonderer Berücksichtigung der Gewebe. *Abhandl. Naturforsch. Gesell. Halle,* IV. pp. 229–250, 1 pl. *1858.*

(Structure of egg, pp. 247–249, fig. 9.)

Lockwood, S.

The Horse-Foot Crab. *Amer. Naturalist,* IV. pp. 257–274, Pl. III. July, *1870.*

(Development of *Limulus Polyphemus.*)

Milne Edwards, Henri.

Recherches relatives au Développement des Limules. **Soc. Philomath. Paris, Extr. des Procès-Verbaux des Séances, 1838,* pp. 125, 126. **L'Institut,* VI. No. 258, p. 397. *1838.* Disciples' Ed. CUVIER's *Règne Animal,* Crustacés, Pl. LXXVI. fig. 2 *h*, 2 *i*. *Hist. Nat. des Crustacés,* III. p. 546. *1840.*

(Young *Limulus* at time of hatching.)

Notice of, in VAN DER HOEVEN's *Recherches sur l'Histoire Naturelle et l'Anatomie des Limules,* p. 44. Leyde, *1838.*

Packard, A. S., Jr.

On the Embryology of *Limulus Polyphemus*. *Amer. Naturalist,* IV. pp. 498–502, figs. 95–100. Oct. *1870.* *Proc. Boston Soc. Nat. Hist.,* XIV. p. 60. Nov. 16, 1870. *Proc. Amer. Assoc. Adv. Sci.,* 19th Meeting (1870), pp. 247–255, 9 figs. *1871.* *Quart. Journ. Microscop. Sci.* [2], XI. pp. 263–267. *1871.*

(Notice of observations given in full in *Mem. Boston Soc. Nat. Hist.,* II. pp. 155–202. *1872.*)

Morphology and Ancestry of the King Crabs. *Amer. Naturalist.* IV. pp. 754–756. Feb. *1871.*

(Abstract of some of the conclusions stated in *Mem. Boston Soc. Nat. Hist.,* II. pp. 155–202. *1872.*)

The Development of *Limulus Polyphemus*. *Mem. Boston Soc. Nat. Hist.*, 11. pp. 155–202, Pl. III.–V. March, *1872*.

Abstract by the author in *Life Histories of the Crustacea and Insects*, *Amer. Nat.*, IX. pp. 589–592, figs. 239–246, Nov. *1875*; *Life Histories of Animals including Man, or Outlines of Comparative Embryology*, New York, *1876*; and in *Zoölogy for Students and General Readers*, pp. 320–323, New York, *1879*.

See also HENRY WOODWARD's *Monograph of the British Fossil Crustacea of the Order Merostomata*, pp. 214–221. London, *1878*.

Farther Observations on the Embryology of *Limulus*, with Notes on its Affinities. *Amer. Naturalist*, VII. pp. 675–678. Nov. *1873*. *Proc. Amer Assoc. Adv. Sci.*, 22d Meeting (1873), Pt. II. pp. 30–32. *1874*.

On the Development of the Nervous System in *Limulus*. *Amer. Naturalist*, IX. pp. 422–424. July, *1875*.

The Anatomy, Histology, and Embryology of *Limulus Polyphemus*. *Anniver. Mem. Boston Soc. Nat. Hist.* *1880*. 45 pp., 7 pl.

(Embryology, pp. 36–40, Pl. I., III., IV.)

Suhm. *See* **Willemoes-Suhm.**

Van Beneden, Édouard.

De la Place que les Limules doivent occuper dans la Classification des Arthropodes d'après leur Développement embryonnaire. *Ann. Soc. Entomol. Belgique*, XV. *Comptes Rendus*, pp. x., xi. 14 Oct. *1871*. *Gervais's Journ. de Zoologie*, I. pp. 41–44. *1872*. *Ann. Mag. Nat. Hist.* [4], IX. pp. 98, 99. Jan. *1872*.

*[Observations on the first Stages of embryonic Development in *Limulus*.] *Tageblatt d. 46er Versamml. deutsch. Naturforsch. u. Aertze in Wiesbaden*, *1873*, p. 58.

Willemoes-Suhm, Rudolf von.

Von der Challenger-Expedition. Nachträge zu den Briefen an C. Th. E. v. Siebold von R. v. Willemoes-Suhm. VIII. *Zeitschr. f. wissensch. Zool.*, XXIX. pp. cix.–cxxxvi. June, *1877*.

(*Limulus* from the Philippine Islands has a free-swimming nauplius larva, p. cxxxii.)

Challenger-Briefe von Rudolf v. Willemoes-Suhm Dr. Phil. 1872–1875. Nach dem Tode des Verfassers herausgegeben von seiner Mutter. Leipzig, *1877*. 180 pp.

(*Limulus rotundicaudatus* does not have a direct development like *L. Polyphemus* but has a nauplius larva, pp. 157, 158. [Letter to Professor Kupffer.])

TRILOBITA.

Barrande, Joachim.

, Système Silurien du Centre de la Bohême. Prague et Paris.

Métamorphoses des Trilobites, I. pp. 257-278, Pl. VII., XLIX., &c. *1852.* I. Suppl., pp. 182-189, Pl. *passim. 1872.*

Cf. A. GERSTAECKER in BRONN's *Klassen und Ordnungen des Thier-Reichs,* V. (Arthropoda), I. Abt., I. Hälfte, pp. 1200-1208, Taf. XLIII., XLVI. Leipzig und Heidelberg, *1879.*

Ford, S. W.

On some Embryonic Forms of Trilobites from the Primordial Rocks at Troy, N. Y. *Amer. Journ. Sci. & Arts* [3], XIII. pp. 265-273, 1 pl. *1877.*

On additional Embryonic Forms of Trilobites from the Primordial Rocks of Troy, N. Y., with Observations on the Genera *Olenellus, Paradoxides,* and *Hydrocephalus. Amer. Journ. Sci.,* XXII. pp. 250-259, 13 cuts. *1881.*

Walcott, C. D.

Note upon the Eggs of the Trilobite. *31st Ann. Rep. N. Y. State Mus. Nat. Hist.,* pp. 66, 67. Albany, *1879.* (Published and distributed in advance of Report, Sept. 20, *1877.*) *Bull. Mus. Comp. Zoöl., at Harvard Coll., in Cambridge,* VIII. p. 216, Pl. IV. figs. 8, 8*a. 1881.*

Fossils of the Utica Slate. *Trans. Albany Inst.,* X. (Printed in advance, June, *1879.*)

Metamorphoses of *Triarthrus Becki,* pp. 24-33, Pl. II. figs. 1-15.

———•———

PYCNOGONIDA.

Allman [George James].

On a Remarkable Form of Parasitism among the *Pycnogonidæ. Rep. Brit. Assoc. Adv. Sci. for* 1859, Trans. of Sect., p. 143. *1860.*

(Young *Ammothea?* parasitic in *Coryne.*)

Böhm, R.

Zwei neue, von Herrn Dr. Hilgendorf in Japan gesammelte Pycnogoniden. *Sitzungs-Ber. Gesell. naturforsch. Freunde zu Berlin,* 1879, pp. 53-60, 140-142.

(On some structural characters of the young, pp. 55, 140, 141.)

Claparède, A. René Edouard.

Beobachtungen über Anatomie und Entwicklungsgeschichte wirbelloser Thiere an der Küste von Normandie angestellt. Leipzig, *1863.* viii+120 pp., 18 pl.

(Development of *Phoxichilidium,* pp. 104, 105, Pl. XVIII. figs. 13, 14.)

Couch, R. Q.

On the Metamorphosis of the Crustaceans, including the *Decapoda, Ento-mostraca*, and *Pycnogonidæ*. *Twelfth Ann. Rep. Roy. Cornwall Polytechnic Soc.*, pp. 17–46, Pl. I. Falmouth, *1844.*

(Young of *Orithyia coccinea* and *Nymphon gracile*, pp. 36, 37. First stage of *Orithyia coccinea*, fig. 13.)

Dohrn, Anton.

Untersuchungen über Bau und Entwickelung der Arthropoden. 2. Ueber Entwickelung und Bau der Pycnogoniden. *Jenaische Zeitschr.,* V. pp. 138–157, Taf. V., VI. *1870.*

(According to Dohrn, the *Pycnogonida* are neither *Arachnida* nor *Crustacea*.)

Neue Untersuchungen über Pycnogoniden. *Mittheil. aus der Zoolog. Station zu Neapel,* I. pp. 28–39. *1878.*

Die Pantopoden des Golfes von Neapel und der angrenzenden Meeres-Abschnitte. Eine Monographie. Herausgegeben von der Zoologischen Station zu Neapel. Leipzig, *1881.* 252 pp., 17 pl. (Fauna und Flora des Golfes von Neapel, III. Monographie.)   .

(Development, pp. 69 *et seqq. Phoxichilidium, Pallene.*)

Gegenbaur, Carl.

Zur Lehre vom Generationswechsel und der Fortpflanzung bei Medusen und Polypen. Würzburg, *1854.* 68 pp., 2 pl.

(*Pycnogonum* developing as a parasite in *Eudendrium*, p. 38, foot-note.)

Gerbe, Z.

Appareils vasculaire et nerveux des Larves des Crustacés marins. *Comptes Rendus de l'Acad. des Sci., Paris,* LXII. pp. 932–937. 23 Apr. *1866.*

(Larva of *Nymphon*, pp. 932, 933, foot-note.)

Trans. by W. S. DALLAS in *Ann. Mag. Nat. Hist.* [3], XVIII. pp. 7–12. *1866.*

Hesse [Eugène].

Mémoire sur des Crustacés rares ou nouveaux des Côtes de France. 24e Art. Description d'un nouveau Crustacé appartenant à l'Ordre des *Pycnogoni-diens* et formant le Genre Oomère, Nob. *Ann. Sci. Nat.* [5], Zool., XX. Art. 5. 18 pp., Pl. VIII. *1874.*

(Contains observations on the larvæ of *Phoxichilidium femoratum* Rathke, and *Nymphon grossipes*.)

Hodge, George.

Observations on a Species of Pycnogon (*Phoxichilidium coccineum* Johnston), with an Attempt to explain the Order of its Development. *Ann. Mag. Nat. Hist.* [3], IX. pp. 33–43, Pl. IV., V. *1862.*

(Development of *Phoxichilidium* in *Coryne*.)

Hoek, P. P. C.

Ueber Pycnogoniden. *Niederländisches Arch. f. Zool.*, III. pp. 235–254, Taf. XV., XVI. *1877*.

(Development of *Pallene*, pp. 239, 240, Taf. XVI. figs. 21, 22.)

Report on the *Pycnogonida* dredged by H. M. S. "Challenger," during the Years 1873–76. 167 pp., 21 pl. Appendix II. Contributions to the Anatomy and Embryology of the *Pycnogonida.* Pp. 100–144, Pl. XIX., XX. *Rep. Sci. Results of the Voyage of H. M. S. "Challenger," during the Years* 1873–76, Zool., III. London, Edinburgh, and Dublin, *1881*.

Kölliker, A.

Beiträge zur Entwicklungsgeschichte wirbelloser Thiere. 1. Ueber die ersten Vorgänge im befruchteten Ei. *Arch. f. Anat., Physiol. u. wissensch. Med.* *1843*, pp. 68–141, Taf. VI., VII.

(Cleavage of egg of *Pycnogonon* total, p. 136.)

Krohn, A.

Notiz über die Eierstöcke der Pycnogoniden. *Schleiden u. Froriep's Notizen,* [3], IX. col. 225, 226. May, *1849*.

(Structure of ovarian egg, col. 226.)

Kroyer, Henrik.

Om Pyknogonidernes Forvandlinger. *Naturhistorisk Tidsskr.*, III. pp. 299–306, Tab. III. *1840*. *Isis*, *1841*, col. 713–717, Taf. III. *Ann. Sci. Nat.* [2], Zool., XVII. pp. 288–292, Pl. IX. B. *1842*. (Trans. by LEREBOULLET.)

In GAIMARD's *Voyages de Commission Scientifique du Nord en Scandinavie, en Laponie au Spitzberg et aux Feröe pendant les Années* 1838, 1839 *et* 1840, *sur la Corvette "La Recherche."* Paris, *1842–45*. Zoologie. Crustacés.

(Young *Pycnogonida,* Pl. XXXIX.)

Lewes, George Henry.

Sea-Side Studies at Ilfracombe, Tenby, the Scilly Isles, and Jersey. Edinburgh and London, *1858*. 414 pp., 7 pl.

(Larva of *Nymphon gracile*, p. 203, Pl. V. fig. 4.)

Semper, Carl.

Ueber Pycnogoniden und ihre in Hydroiden schmarotzenden Larvenformen. *Arbeit. aus dem zoolog.-zootom. Inst. in Würzburg*, I. pp. 264–286, Taf. XVI., XVII. *1874*. *Verhandl. d. physikal.-medicin. Gesell. in Würzburg*, [2], VII. pp. 257–279, Taf. IV., V. *1874*.

Wilson, Edmund B.

Synopsis of the *Pycnogonida* of New England. *Trans. Conn. Acad.*, V. pp. 1–26, Pl. I.–VII. *1878*.

(Young of *Achelia spinosa*, p. 8, Pl. II. fig. 1 *g*; of *Nymphon hirtum*, p. 23, Pl. VI. figs. 2 *i*, 2 *j*.)

Report on the *Pycnogonida* of New England and Adjacent Waters. In *Rep. U. S. Commissioner of Fish and Fisheries for* 1878, pp. 463–506, 7 pl. Washington, *1880*.

> (Young of *Achelia spinosa*, p. 474; of *Nymphon hirtum*, p. 496, Pl. VII. fig. 41, as before.)

Reports on the Results of Dredging, under the Supervision of Alexander Agassiz, along the East Coast of the United States, during the Summer of 1880, by the U. S. Coast Survey Steamer " Blake," Commander J. R. Bartlett, U. S. N., commanding. XIII. Report on the *Pycnogonida*. *Bull. Mus. Comp. Zoöl., at Harvard Coll., in Cambridge,* VIII. pp 239–256, 5 pl. *1881*.

> (Development of *Pallene* shows that Zenker's account of the innervation of the three anterior pairs of appendages of *Pycnogonida* is incorrect, p. 241, footnote.)

Wright, T. Strethill.

Observations on British Zoöphytes.   9. On the Development of Pycnogon Larvæ within the Polyps of *Hydractinia echinata*.   *Quart. Journ. Microscop. Sci.* [2], III. pp. 51, 52.   *1863*.

www.ingramcontent.com/pod-product-compliance
Lightning Source LLC
Chambersburg PA
CBHW030900260626
47169CB00008B/2609